Times Square and Other Stories

TIMES SQUARE

AND OTHER STORIES

BY

William Baer

ABLE MUSE PRESS

Able Muse Press

www.ablemusepress.com

Printed in the United States of America

Library of Congress Control Number: 2014950256

ISBN 978-1-927409-43-5 (paperback)
ISBN 978-1-927409-44-2 (digital)

Cover image: "Appointed Place" by Alexander Pepple

Cover & book design by Alexander Pepple

Able Muse Press is an imprint of *Able Muse:* A Review of Poetry, Prose & Art—at
www.ablemuse.com

Able Muse Press
467 Saratoga Avenue #602
San Jose, CA 95129

For my family and friends—

especially Maggie

Acknowledgments

I am grateful to the editors of the following journals where a number of these stories originally appeared, sometimes in variant versions:

Kansas Quarterly:	"Disumbrationism"
Mississippi Valley Review:	"Endgame"
The Dalhousie Review:	"The Plagiarist"
The Chariton Review:	"Pure Cinema"
The Iowa Review:	"Shroud"
Trajectory:	"Times Square"

CONTENTS

I come to you not as a gravedigger, but as a diagnostician.

– Russell Kirk

Times Square and Other Stories

NEW YORK CITY (AND ENVIRONS)

Times Square

AT EXACTLY 2:15 PM, SEPTEMBER 29TH, as predestinated, he turned left at the corner of West Forty-Second Street and Seventh Avenue, moving comfortably within the rapid ebbs-and-flows of the thousands of pedestrians streaming past and the nearby cabs and cars racing down Seventh Avenue. As he entered into the square, he stared up at the all-encompassing signage, most specifically those massive, moving, illuminated "spectaculars," as they're known these days, with their dazzling, endless, brightly flashing, kaleidoscopic colors.

Then he looked across the street at Times Square One, and he saw her standing and waiting beneath the exact spot where each-and-every brand-new year begins, where the glittering Times Square "ball" slowly descends, not quite to the sidewalk, in the waning moments of each passing year, and she wore a rather stunning, sleek red dress, with black shoes, a matching black-leather bag, and a red, exactly the same color, lightweight cotton coat, which was casually draped over her left arm. She was remarkably lovely, even in ways that he'd certainly not expected. Her hair was long and dark, and she definitely had a "Latin" look of some kind, certainly more than most of the New York City girls who were gliding past—or maybe it was actually a "Mediterranean" look of some kind.

At the streetlight, he walked across Seventh to where she was standing, and he asked her, as instructed, as preordained, his undeniably foolish question.

"Is this Times Square?"

> *To actually "be" the story's (shall-we-say) protagonist, you already have to "be," at least, all of the following: (which is, of course, just like life, not really fair at all, but which is, nevertheless, exactly what he is and was) a native Argentine, preferably Buenos Aires, or (also acceptable) a native of any other South American country, south of the Guajira Peninsula: trim, lean, tallish, fit, darkish, attractive, neat, polite, somewhere between twenty-five and thirty-two years old, university educated, and, presently, visiting the United States for the first time, with a workable (communicating) facility with the English language, and specifically dressed as follows. . . . [AH]*

She turned and looked.

He was, as she was pleased to see, quite handsome, a bit formalish in his manner, carrying a rather unnecessary black umbrella, and certainly more-than-a-bit mysterious as well, which, she supposed, was to be fully expected under the circumstances, yet clearly not the naturally anticipated "Anglo" type, being hardly a "Yankee," but maybe, instead, a dark-eyed Cuban, or a dark-eyed Puerto Rican. Or maybe, given his rather exacting Spanish accent, he'd come from much farther south, maybe even south of the Equator. Maybe even Argentina. Or Chile. He wore an impeccably tailored black suit, with gleaming-new black shoes, a white dress shirt, and a thin-ish red tie, which might, or might not, have matched the exact color of her dress.

"Yes, Times Square," she said, also fully intoxicated by the sensate whirl of the place and the time and the moment in the midst of this whirling, bustling, vibrant crossroads of the world. "It's very beautiful."

He nodded.

"Yes, it's like the Aleph," he said.

And she knew exactly *what* that was, because she'd come prepared, and she smiled, almost laughed, and he looked deepishly into her eyes, as if fascinated, as if the whirl of the stupendous flashing city was now flashing across the surface of her eyes, concealing whatever lay beneath, and he added, "As are your eyes."

Yes, you can read this, of course, as anyone can, as you are, in fact, doing right now, at this very moment, reading this overlong sentence, and you can, again, as, of course, anyone can, identify yourself with the "you" you've just encountered, just as we've all done before, "becoming," even, in a sense, "being," at different moments in our lives, Jane Eyre and Ishmael and Funes and Lucia Mondella, and yet, both within-and-without the "linguistic" confines of this present unfolding story, only those of you who are "exactly" like "you," can fully "live" the story fully, especially after it's read.

So I will assume, from this point forward, that you are "you" and that you are lovely—which is something that all women just "know," knowing whether we are, or whether we aren't, being also fully aware that being so, or not being so, is either a providential gift or a providential injustice that's both irreparable and unappealable—and "you" are also naturally elegant, especially with your movements, and svelte, and capable of "carrying off" the red dress (details below), being also a native of Italy, either north or south, or from any of the Mediterranean countries from Algeciras to Athens, including Southern France, at least twenty-three years old, but not yet over thirty, well-read, well-educated, well-adjusted, both stable and generally upbeat, a believer in love and providence and fate, fluent, or, at least, quasi-fluent, in the English language, and now visiting both America and New York for the very first time, and then, when dressed as detailed below, on the date given below, at the exact time given below, he appears amid the endless crowds and lights and streaming cars and noises and wonders and confusions of Times Square and politely asks you a foolish question, you'll respond accordingly, also politely, and then add that it's all very "beautiful," which you must believe in your heart, and then he will look in your eyes and respond with a simile of some kind. . . . [IS]

Then he decided.

As if casually, as if almost imperceptively, as if it wasn't the most important decision of his life, which it was, which he knew without a doubt.

"Could we walk a bit?" he asked.

And then, right then, right there, if, for whatever reason, something's not quite right, if, despiting all the money you've spent, and all the time and foolish hopes you've already invested, and no matter how much you might, suddenly, be angered by your own pathetic stupidity and self-delusion, you must, once again, very politely, with a smile, say, "Have a lovely day," and end the story right there, at least your version of the story, because she, just like you, is also hopeful and fragile and taking a tremendous risk, so you must be kind and gentle and think only of her. But, if, on the other hand, you feel that it feels just right, that this is exactly what's destined to be, beginning right here, in this peculiar place, in the teeming

heart of the Empire City, in the swirling, humming, buzzing,
confusing, hyper-stimulated overload of the skyscraper city,
then simply ask, "Could we walk a bit?" [AH]

"I'd like that," she responded with a smile, and he clearly recognized and was fully charmed by her Italianate accent.

Together, they crossed at the stoplight to the west side of Seventh Avenue and walked north amid the crowds, amid the New Yorkers, amid the tourists, amid the lovely September sunshine, as if they were all alone.

And when he asks you if he might accompany you on a walk
through the Square, you must be true, you must be honest,
and you must decide—which, more often than not, we women
can do better than "them"—for we know, as if instinctively,
the devastating power we have, and we know, as a natural
consequence, that it's always kinder to simply and politely
refuse, to smile and say "No," or to smile and say "I'm sorry,
but I can't," rather than encourage their foolish hopes—even
though you yourself are fully aware that it was only your own
foolish hopes that somehow led you to be presently standing
there alone at Times Square One and talking to a stranger.
If, however, on the other hand, he seems to be what you've
been looking for, and hoping for, and praying for, then simply
smile and say, "I'd like that." [IS]

"So how did you end up here today?" she asked, finding it hard to believe that she was saying what she was saying, saying exactly what she'd been instructed to say.

So he told her.

He explained that for the past three years, he'd been taking care of his younger brother in Campana, forty-five miles northwest of Buenos Aires. He explained that his brother Carlos, a rather free-spirited university student at the time, had wrecked his young life in an almost-fatal motorcycle crash in the Recoleta. His spine had been crushed and there'd been severe head trauma and brain damage. After six months in a Buenos Aires hospital and numerous operations, he (the stranger now walking through Times Square) and his mother had moved Carlos to Campana, where they took care of him for three years until he finally died from the repercussions of the crash, leaving behind a copy of *Dieciséis Tangos*.

Which was a curious collection of sixteen short stories by Antonio Hernández, a reputable and somewhat well-known Argentine novelist, who'd published the collection in Buenos Aires in 1964, and, for some reason, the third story in Carlos's edition, a story entitled *"Istruzioni,"* was starred with a pen-marked asterisk on the contents page, and Carlos had also written right next to the story's title, in his rather unstable brain-damaged script, the words, *"Para mi hermano—¿Por qué no?,"* meaning, "For my Brother—Why not?" So the stranger had read the story, as his brother had clearly wished, and then he read it again, and many other times, subsequently reconsidering his entire life and finally asking himself, "Why not?" Then he checked his finances, made the travel arrangements, read "El Aleph," and flew to New York City.

When she asks you "why" you are there, tell the truth, of course. Tell her that you read this story, and that, for whatever your own "personal" reasons (give them, explain them), you felt compelled to travel to New York City and come to Times Square. It will, of course, be impossible not to feel a little bit embarrassed about the rather ludicrous nature of your actions, but that's to be expected. Keep in mind that "she"

(the one walking next to you) is also here for some, as yet,
unknown unfathomable reason, and now you can ask her
yourself. [AH]

So she explained that she'd come back to Castello from
Ethiopia infected with a rare zoonotic virus, and that her family
had arranged for her recuperation at an aunt's home in Dorgali
on the eastern coast of Sardinia, where she began reading fiction
again, quite voraciously, eventually discovering on her Aunt Lenora's
bookshelves a peculiar collection of stories by Isabella Sorella, an
apparently forgotten Roman writer, who'd published her oddish
collection in Milan in 1965.

It was entitled *Racconti mai detti prima,* and it included a
story entitled *"Una mappa di amore,"* which she found perfectly
mesmerizing since it seemed more like a "directive," *una mappa,*
than a short story, and since she was well within the multiple
"parameters" of the "you" in Sorella's story, she began to fantasize
about it, and think to herself, "Now wouldn't that be nice?" and
"Wouldn't that be fun to try, even though it's, of course, perfect
nonsense?" And when she was fully recuperated, although still
completely uncertain about her own life and her own future, she
returned to her parents' home in Castello and decided to visit
another aunt (her Aunt Angelina), who lived somewhere in some
place called New Jersey, so that she could come to Times Square
today, exactly as directed, and let whatever-would-happen, happen.

When he's told you why he's here, then you need to tell him
why you're here as well. Not your entire history, that will,
of course, come in time, but why you're here right now, why
you're presently walking through Times Square with a red
dress and a stranger. [IS]

At Forty-Sixth Street, they crossed Broadway to the south end of Duffy Square, each feeling simultaneously amazed and embarrassed by everything that was happening. Beneath the bronze statue of Francis Duffy, always imposing in his Army trench coat, they paused a moment.

"I'd like to show you something," she said.

At the north end of the Square, beneath the statue, she'll "propose" something, and you will, of course, agree. [AH]

"Of course," he said, knowing exactly what to do.

He hailed a cab, and when they got into the backseat, the cabbie turned around, and he looked at her, and she remembered exactly what she needed to remember:

"Sixth and Central Park South," she said, and the cabbie nodded, turned, and they were off.

Enter the park through the Artist's Gate at Sixth Street. Enjoy the park in September, and if there's some falling rain, enjoy that as well from beneath his umbrella. Then casually lead him to the statue of José de San Martín, which he'll much appreciate. Then roam aimlessly about the south end of the park, maybe buying some ice cream, maybe sitting on a bench and talking about yourselves, about who you are, about what you love, about what you dream about. Don't be afraid. It's too late for that now. [IS]

He looked up at the spectacular statue of the great General, who sat, majestic, astride his military horse, pointing off into the ineffable distance, and it would, of course, be impossible to describe his pleasure, seeing the great liberator, the great freedom-fighter, honored right here, in the heart of this bizarre city, within its beautiful central park. The statue, as he could see at a glance, was clearly a recast, yet somewhat smaller version of the magnificent statue that dominated the Plaza San Martín in the Retiro section of Buenos Aires, not far from where he'd once lived. For him, as an Argentine, and also as a trained historian, it was especially powerful to see this unexpected tribute to the great Captain of the Andes, but, then again, as he well appreciated, *anyone* born-and-raised south of the Guajira Peninsula, would have appreciated it as well, since San Martín had not only liberated Argentina, and Chile, and Peru, but he was also, like Bolivar, universally admired—but even more so.

Then they strolled deeper into the park, and he bought them both a strawberry ice cream cone, and they sat on a bench overlooking the pond, just as *"Istruzioni"* had instructed, and he told her his name, and he answered all of her questions.

His name was Miguel César Mendoza.

He was twenty-nine, and he'd been born in Buenos Aires, not far from the Catedral Metropolitana, where the earthly remains of San Martín lay within a huge black sarcophagus in a mausoleum located off to the right side of the right aisle, attended by a perpetual military honor guard. Miguel's now-deceased father had been an architect, and his mother was still a librarian and, as everyone who knew her concurred, a saint as well. Miguel attended the Universidad de Buenos Aires, majored in history, specifically the War of the Triple Alliance, almost married Rosalita Delgado, and was enrolled in the university's doctorate program when his brother drank too many *aguardientes* in Recoleta and smashed his bike, an American Harley, into a railway trestle.

Miguel promptly dropped out of graduate school to assist his mother, and they spent over three years attending to the needs of Carlos at the family's rural cottage in Campana on the Paraná River. When his brother had died in his sleep two months ago, Miguel was devastated, which was both unexpected and inexplicable, considering that his brother's death had long been anticipated. But he'd, suddenly, felt particularly "lost" and purposeless and certainly unable and unprepared to resume his studies. Then he stumbled onto the Hernández story left behind by his brother, and he decided to submit himself, with exactitude, to the instructions in *"Istruzioni."*

> *Then it will be your turn to listen. And to ask whatever you'd like to ask. [AH]*

Her name was Francesca Savelli.

She was born, twenty-eight years ago, in Città di Castello, thirty-seven miles north of Assisi, in the town made famous by Margaret of Castello, the Dominican Mantellate who died in 1320 and who still lay preserved under the high altar of Chiesa di San Domenico. Like her father, and the two younger sisters who would follow her lead, Francesca had never wanted to be anything else in life but a physician, and she'd received her medical degree from the Università degli Studi di Milano three years ago.

Then, to the dismay of her ever-loving parents and sisters, who never even knew about her recently terminated and deeply hurtful romance with a fellow medical student, Francesca decided to go to Africa and work amid the dispossessed in Ethiopia. She was not, as she convinced herself at the time, simply running away from love, or from love lost, because she'd *always* had the intention to dedicate at least a portion of her life in service to the destitute, but whatever she told herself, whatever her self-justifications, she knew, within her heart, that she really was running away from her life—at least for the time being. Then two years ago, when she contracted an extremely rare and dangerous zoonotic virus, she was sent back to Castello, and her sister Gregoria, now a pathology specialist, took her to their aunt's home in Sardinia for what turned out to be a twelve-month recuperation. . . .

When Francesca finished talking about herself, Miguel was perfectly pleased and silent.

Then she asked him a question.

"What about love?"

"I believe," Miguel explained, without hesitation, "exactly what Hernández wrote in his story—because I've *always* believed it—long before I read it in 'Istruzioni.'"

Francesca waited.

Then Miguel recited the exact lines that he'd both translated and memorized for this very moment.

"Love, of course, can be many things, but if it doesn't begin with submission, then it really isn't love. One must be willing and eager to submit oneself to the one one loves."

Francesca was pleased, and she nodded, agreeing with Hernández, agreeing with Miguel, and agreeing with what she'd always felt in her heart.

> *Don't be afraid. Don't be afraid to ask about love. Why else are you there?* [IS]

Then, rather unexpectedly, Miguel stood up and recited, as instructed, an old-fashioned love poem—which had been cited in the original Spanish story, being, oddly enough, its only English-language section—a poem for which Hernández had given neither author nor date, neither origin nor reference, possibly implying that the poem was one of his own creations, or maybe an English translation of one of his own Spanish sonnets, assuming that he'd ever written poems and sonnets.

It began, "Blessed be the day, the month, and the year" and it ended, ". . . and every thought of mine/ is only of her, and shared with no one else." Which seemed a bit odd to Miguel, who couldn't fathom why—under the present circumstances—it was appropriate, given that it was written in the voice of one who'd already loved his love for a very long time, although he (Miguel) still recited it with both sincerity and conviction.

And from the first few words, it was perfectly clear that it gave Francesca an inordinate pleasure and satisfaction since—as she'd soon explain—it was a reasonably accurate English translation of Petrarch's famous sonnet 61, *"Benedetto sia 'l giorno, e 'l mese, et l'anno . . . ,"* which Liszt had set to music sometime in the 1880s, and which she'd memorized as a young schoolgirl in Castello, and which she promptly recited in the original Italian while still sitting on her bench in Central Park.

Naturally, Miguel was delighted, perfectly pleased with her pleasure, and when Francesca finished, he wondered out loud:

"I wonder if Hernández translated the poem himself?"

"I bet he did," Francesca guessed and smiled and shrugged, and they seemed perfectly comfortable with each other, both fascinated and even playfully intimate.

Then Francesca looked into her black-leather purse, pulled out a small recorder, and played a song that she'd obviously prerecorded for this exact and specific moment. It was an old song by a forgotten American group called The Dubs, which began with its title, which apparently contained no question mark: "Could This Be Magic."

Miguel, still standing and listening, held out his hand.

"Could we dance?" he asked.

As if on cue.

Francesca, although clearly surprised, didn't even bother to say, "I'm really not much of a dancer," or something like that, which wasn't true anyway, and she took his hand, and they touched for the very first time, and she stood up, and he stepped gently towards her, and they embraced for the very first time, and it was truly, as the song speculated, "magical," even though they both knew that it was also, on the surface of things, perfectly ludicrous, but they didn't care. They were content. They were, in truth, in reality, far more than simply "content," as they slowly moved, together and closely, in the beautiful park, in this strangely beautiful city, to the smooth smooth tenor of Richard Blandon and the lovely harmonics of the other four Dubs.

> *When you hear a song in the park, a slow song, a love song, a lovely song, don't hesitate. Ask her to dance. Hold her tenderly, as you would hold the most precious thing on earth. [AH]*

When the song ended, they again sat down on the bench.

"That was very beautiful," he said, and she agreed, and she nodded. "I suppose it was in your story?" he supposed. "In Sorella's story?"

"Yes, it was," she explained, "but I'm not sure why—and I have no idea why Sorella was so specific about that particular song."

"What exactly *is* it?" Miguel wondered.

"It's something they once called Doo-Wop," she explained, having looked it up. "It was a kind of mellow, harmonic style that was apparently very popular in the early days of rock and roll."

They both smiled, and they both shrugged.

"Well, whatever it is, and whatever it means," Miguel decided, "it's very beautiful."

So they talked some more.

They talked about many things, both significant and frivolous, about her love of children and chocolate bonbons and tennis and Renaissance art and forgotten novenas, and about his love of the tango and the songs of Carlos Gardel and film noirs and formula-one racing and Swiss milk chocolate and much much more.

Then Miguel checked his watch.

"Is it 5:00?" she wondered, fully aware that that particular time was particularly significant, and, quite naturally, she wondered what was next.

"Yes," Miguel said.

"Do you know what we're supposed to do?" she asked.

"Yes," he said.

So they strolled back to Central Park South, and Miguel hailed another taxi.

> *Talk freely, talk honestly, talk about whatever you wish. Enjoy yourself. [IS]*

The taxi stopped at 476 Fifth Avenue, and they immediately went up the stairs, between the resting lions, and entered the New York Public Library. At the Special Collections desk on the third floor, Miguel spoke to the librarian.

"We'd like to see the signed copy of Borges's *Cuentos de Uqbar*, 1957, limited edition. Reference number B-826549."

The silent librarian wrote down the necessary information, nodded politely, and left the desk.

As they waited in the library silence, Francesca whispered.

"Can you tell me what we're supposed to do?"

"Of course," Miguel explained. "We're supposed to sign our names on the inside of the back cover."

Then Miguel just shrugged, and Francesca smiled.

"As if to record our meeting?" she wondered out loud.

"I suppose so," Miguel agreed, with obvious uncertainty.

Then the librarian returned, carrying a dark binder, which she immediately opened on the desk in front of her, revealing the extremely rare first-and-only edition, which seemed to be in excellent condition, along with a dark ballpoint pen and a half-sheet of red paper with the word, "NOTE," printed across the top in large bold letters. The librarian picked up the short note, read it quickly, looked at Francesca and Miguel with an unconcealed curiosity, and said:

"Come with me."

> *Enter within the great library, which makes us all, forever and always, realize exactly how much "nothing" we really know, and, of course, enjoy her company, and think how fortunate you are to be there with her, alone, together. [AH]*

They immediately followed the elderly lady through a series of interior corridors to a small bookless, shelfless reading room with darkly paneled walls. Then the librarian placed *Cuentos de Uqbar* on the old wooden table and placed the black pen right next to it.

"When you're done," the librarian instructed, "please press the button."

Then she nodded at a little white button located on the wall nearest the table, and she left the room. When she was gone,

Francesca and Miguel sat down in the two waiting chairs, and Francesca opened the small book to the title page, and she read out loud the handwritten dedication, which was neatly printed in English:

"For Antonio, who is cleverer than Borges, and maybe even cleverer than Macedonio, which is, of course, *impossible.*"

Signed: "Borges."

"Did you know," Francesca wondered, "that they knew each other?"

"No," Miguel admitted. "They both lived in Buenos Aires, of course, but they were definitely from different generations." Then he thought of something else. "Let's check the contents."

Carefully, Francesca turned to the contents page, and *there* it was, seemingly perfectly content and comfortable amid a number of other Borges fictions.

"*There* it is," they both said, as if in unison, staring down at the fifth story in the collection, "The Aleph," first published in *Sur* in 1945, which they'd both been required to read, about some inexplicable "thing," the "Aleph," which was located in somebody's basement on Garay Street in Buenos Aires, and which, if observed in exactly the right way, would reveal, in a single stupendous instant, every single thing that was then taking place everywhere on the planet earth—the place where *all* the places are—or, at least, where all the places can be seen.

"This is fun," Francesca admitted, and she looked at Miguel playfully. "Should we sign the book?"

"I'm ready," Miguel agreed with a smile.

So Francesca turned to the very back of the book, and they were stunned to see all the names and the dates, beginning with "Isabella Sorella & Antonio Hernández—1958."

"Were they lovers?" Francesca wondered out loud.

"Maybe the stories are true?" Miguel wondered out loud.

"Maybe they *really* did meet on September 15, 1958 at 2:15?" Francesca hypothesized.

"At Forty-Second and Seventh," Miguel added.

"And that would explain the music," Francesca continued. "Maybe they were walking through the park, and some kid was playing a radio, and 'Could This Be Magic' came on, and they started to dance?"

"And then later," Miguel continued, "*much* later, maybe they agreed to write the two stories to try and recreate the moment for others. For the kinds of people who would be crazy enough, just like us, to do what they were told in a piece of literary fiction."

Then Miguel looked down at the book and pointed at all the names.

"And *these* are the names of all the crazy people," he said, as Francesca looked them over as well.

"There must be fifty names," she estimated, "maybe twenty-five couples."

"Let's count," Miguel suggested, which they did, in unison, with Francesca pointing at each entry, at each paring, until they finished with "34."

"And look," she pointed out, "there are, as you'd expect, some missing years, but back in 1978, there are two entries! Two couples!"

"Which explains," Miguel remembered, "why Hernández wrote in *"Istruzioni,"* that "if, as would be most unlikely, as would actually be absurd, you see two different women dressed in red at Times Square One, then approach the one who is closest, and never look at the other one again."

"This is nuts!" Francesca laughed, making no attempt to contain her obvious delight.

"Yes, it is," Miguel agreed.

Then she looked into his dark Argentine eyes.

"Are you ready to sign?"

"More than anything else," Miguel assured her.

So right below "Margherita Borelli & Juan Pablo Ramírez," Francesca carefully wrote her name (and the ampersand) with the black pen, which she handed to Miguel, who signed his name just as neatly and carefully.

Then he looked at Francesca.

"Now what?" he smiled.

"I have an idea," she said, and she pushed the white button.

When the librarian returned, which seemed almost immediately, Francesca asked the older woman, "Can you tell us what's written on the red piece of paper?"

"Of course," the librarian assured her, "as a matter of fact, I'm obligated to do so."

So she read the note out loud:

"To the on-duty librarian: As part of our obligation upon receiving this rare and valuable donation from Señor Antonio Hernández in 1958, we are instructed as follows: If a woman in a red dress, accompanied by a man in a black suit, request to see this book on September 29th, of any year, on the feast of the archangel Azarias (or on the subsequent Monday if that date falls on a Sunday), they will not only be allowed to peruse the collection, but also to sign their names inside the back cover with the enclosed black pen used by Señor Borges himself to inscribe the volume in 1957. There's no need to instruct them to do so since they already know what to do. When they've done so, and when they're ready to leave, you will read them this note and remind them to read the 'bios.' Thank you."

"Does any of this make sense?" the librarian asked with a rather baffled smile.

"I think it does," Miguel added. Then he turned to Francesca, "I think it means the bios of the authors—the bios of Sorella and Hernández."

Francesca agreed.

"Maybe they were married?" she wondered.

"But I've already checked into Hernández," Miguel pointed out, with obvious disappointment, "and his wife's name was María."

Then, just before they left the room, the librarian asked:

"Did you meet today?"

"Yes," Miguel answered.

Then the older lady smiled again, quite mischievously.

"Do you know the other name of Azarias?" she asked, as if the name was just one of those innumerable facts that a librarian might or might not know.

"Yes," answered Francesca immediately, "Raphael."

Which Miguel didn't know.

The librarian nodded and explained:

"He's the patron of lovers, and marriage—and of happy meetings."

The might-be lovers were stunned.

"Like Tobias?" Miguel wondered.

"Exactly," the librarian assured him.

A few minutes later, downstairs in the Reference section, sitting next to each other, each sitting before a keyboard and an active computer screen, it was, naturally, much easier to find out information about Sr. Antonio Hernández:

Born in Buenos Aires in 1926, he was the son of an Argentine diplomat and his Brazilian wife. At the Universidad de Buenos Aires, where he studied literature, Hernández was a very close friend of Hector Fernandez, the grandson of Macedonio Fernandez, the literary "mentor" of J.L. Borges. As a result, Hernández had not only met Macedonio, but he'd also met the leading literary lights of the intervening generation: Borges, Adolfo Bioy Casares, the Ocampo sisters, etc.

After graduation, Hernández left Argentina to spend three years in Brazil helping his father lay the groundwork for the new Argentine Embassy for the newly forming capital of Brasilia. While he was still living on the Planalto Central, Hernández's first novel, *Iguazu,* was published in Buenos Aires to enthusiastic reviews. As a result, he was invited to a reception in honor of the book's success at the Argentine Embassy in New York City in 1958, which Borges attended. During his trip to Manhattan, Hernández met his future wife, although there were no specific details in any of the web sources about their meeting.

"Look, you were right!" Miguel said, pointing at the screen. "María was Isabella's middle name."

So they read the text together:

"Hernández and his Italian wife, María (the writer Isabella María Sorella) were married in early 1959 in Castello, Italy, but they lived in Buenos Aires for the rest of their lives, raising three children. The most notable of Hernández's subsequent and various works were *El borde del mundo, El jaguar,* and *La mujer de mi sueño.* He died in Campana in 1994 of heart failure."

Locating information about Isabella María Sorella, as Francesca had already learned in Castello, was much harder, probably because her output was so small, probably because she was essentially apolitical, probably because she preferred the short story to the novel, and probably because she'd eventually decided to move away from Europe. But, recently, there'd been a handful of Italian writers and critics who'd rediscovered and then reconsidered her peculiarly crafted stories, and, as a result, Francesca was able to piece together a few helpful sources which she translated on-the-spot to share with Miguel:

Isabella María Sorella was born in Rome in 1929. Her father was a math professor at La Sapienza, and both he and his wife doted on their daughter, their only child, and encouraged her almost compulsive desire to be a writer. Eventually Isabella studied languages at La Sapienza, worked as a translator at the Vatican, and published a number of short stories in various Italian literary journals, mostly of the avant-garde type, although her work was hard to classify, being plot-obsessed, quirkily syntaxed, yet highly readable.

One of those early stories, appropriately titled *"La trama,"* she translated into English, mailed overseas to *The Greenwich Review,* a quite prestigious New York literary journal in its day, and the story was accepted for publication. In her subsequent correspondence with the journal's editor, Jason Allan Howard, he'd written, apparently with sincerity, "If you ever come to New York, please come and visit me—and my family—in Manhattan." So she did, in September 1958, where she met Antonio Hernández. Apparently, for the rest of her life, she continued to write occasional stories, always oddly premised and carefully crafted, until her death from cancer in Argentina in 1996.

Then Francesca and Miguel shut down their respective search engines and sat pensively in the silence of the huge and endless library.

"They must have loved each other very much," Francesca decided.

"Yes," Miguel agreed.

Then they both thought about that particular *kind* of lasting love in the ensuing silence.

Francesca smiled.

"In my story," she explained to Miguel, "you're now supposed to ask me to dinner."

Miguel smiled as well.

"Yes," he remembered, "and in my story it said exactly where."

"Where?"

"The Waldorf-Astoria," he said, and she was obviously pleased. So they left the library behind, taking yet another cab to 301 Park Avenue.

When they arrived, Miguel asked Francesca to pick one of the Waldorf's restaurants, just as Hernández has directed, and soon, over Miguel's soup and over Francesca's salad, they read each other's stories.

> *When he takes you to dinner, give him a copy of this story, translated into English, to read over his soup. [IS]*

Two years ago in Sardinia, when Francesca had read that particular directive, she'd wondered, "I wonder what the 'you' is supposed to do while he's reading this story?"

But now she knew.

> *Once you're comfortably settled at your table in the Waldorf, offer her a copy, in English, of this story, even if you have to translate it yourself. [AH]*

So he did.

So they read together, separately.

And Miguel most appreciated the short section in *"Una mappa di amore"* that read:

> *You will naturally wonder if it's possible that a lasting indelible love could come of such a "chance" meeting, especially one that wasn't really chance. You will naturally wonder, "Could someone really meet someone in Times Square and never love anyone else ever again? And the answer is yes. [IS]*

And Francesca especially liked the section in *"Istruzioni"* which read:

> *You will find yourself vacillating back-and-forth between thinking that this is all some kind of insanely manipulated delusion or that it's, most likely, the most wonderful thing that will ever happen in your entire life. Only one can be true. [AH]*

When dinner was over, and all their talk about this-and-that in the stories and about this-and-that in their own lives was finished, they walked arm-in-arm the nine blocks to the St. Regis, where she'd been instructed to stay by Isabella Sorella. They remained mostly silent—contented like young children satiated with dessert, like satisfied lovers who've both decided that there's nothing more that could be said or done on September 29, except to hold each other and think about the future.

Which they did, and which they were still doing under the St. Regis awning at Fifty-Fifth and Fifth, when they looked into each other's eyes and Francesca asked:

"Can we do this every day?"

And if he says, "Yes," you will ask, "For the rest of our lives?"
and if he says, "Yes" once again, then you will allow him
to kiss you, tenderly, once, before you retire alone into your
Beaux-Art salon, amid the marbles and the silk-covered
walls, and the opulent chandeliers, to prepare yourself to
face the next day, September 30th, and your entire future
for that matter, totally unguided, without a map, without
directions, without instructions, without me—but not, of
course, entirely alone. [IS]

"Yes."

"For the rest of our lives?" she wondered, as Miguel knew
she would, having just read her story at the Waldorf.

"Yes."

So they kissed each other, gently, inevitably, ever-too-briefly,
and then they came apart, and Francesca retired into the lobby
of the St. Regis, and he watched her go, and he wanted to run
after her, and hold her again, and keep her up all night, and make
all kinds of promises, and even talk about marriage, but he did
exactly as he'd been told.

When she walks into the lobby, you will feel the urge to
rush after her, but you need to let her go. You need to be
satisfied with today, with the first day, with this auspicious
beginning. Then you need to stay up all night and think
about how good you'll be to her for the rest of your life. [AH]

Francesca let him kiss her, tenderly, and she wanted more,
but she turned around and went to her designated suite on the
elegant fifteenth floor and looked out the window at the glittering

lights of the Empire City, and she thought about him down there, somewhere, doing nothing but thinking about her, and also thinking about:

> *And when he's gone, at some point, you'll surely think about us, the first "Times Square" lovers, who are, quite possibly, by now, long dead-and-gone and silent in our side-by-side graves in la Chacarita—pray for us—and you will probably think about us plotting and planning the future, your future, without even knowing who you are, and then, you might even think back to 1958, [fill in the number] years ago, when I was a young woman standing alone in Times Square wearing a red dress when a handsome young man came up to me and asked me a ridiculous question, and I fell in love. [IS]*

Disumbrationism

S HE HAD, APPARENTLY, STOOD FOR MOST of the late afternoon in that gently lit but windowless room of the gallery's interior. Her soft-white clothes were strikingly attractive; she wore ribbons in her hair, and a delicately flowing dress with faint blue trim. She stood, I'm told, impassive and immobile, oblivious to those around her, and, despite the overwhelming charm of her appearance, she was clearly disturbed by a deep and unstable inner turmoil: a confusion and a mounting anxiety. At closing, as one of the elderly guards cautiously approached, she raised a small, flashing, silver knife from her purse, and, almost instinctively, struck out violently at the canvas before her—slitting open the upper left-hand corner of Malevich's 1918 study "Suprematist Composition: White on White." She then turned to the stunned guard and said softly, with a certain tragic resignation, "They've abandoned all care for the beautiful."

It was now two years since her arrest, and as I walked up the Modern's west staircase and passed through the "Early Geometric Abstract" exhibit (Room 18), I thought again of that young girl, my natural sympathy for her convictions, and, although I'd prefer not to admit it, a certain admiration for her actions. Walking

31

past the work of Pevsner, Moholy-Nagy, and through the "Early Abstract Expressionists," Kupka, Delaunay, and Kandinsky, it was easy to succumb to such "romantic" notions that art in our century had failed in a perverse, intentional, and, as Ortega had once described, "dehumanizing" fashion.

Her name, I remember, was Charlotte Spenser, and I wrote her at the time, unaware that she'd given at least a false name and quite possibly a false address. I was concerned about her instability and its intensity, and I felt a deep commiseration with her concerns and purpose. The Modern, of course, handled the "unfortunate" incident in the most "civilized" manner; they dropped the charges and admitted no publicity. On the same evening of the slashing, they'd called NYU's International Foundation for Art Research, and I was sent over to package the picture and bring it back to the lab for immediate restoration. The overwhelming folly of "restoring" such shallow and talentless abstraction—a picture which the gallery, as it admits in its catalog, is uncertain how to properly hang (that is: which side is up)—did not deter a thorough and perfectly invisible mending of the damage, but I continued to be repulsed by the Modern itself, feeling that it was a monumental tabernacle to man's most pretentious and fraudulent impulses, and I assiduously avoided the place for over two years.

But now I was back again, for the curious reason that someone had found it amusing to write an anonymous and menacing letter to the curator claiming that one of its pictures was nothing but an ingenious copy. Normally, since my status at the foundation was now secure, I refused any involvement with works of the twentieth century, except for those few exceptions I myself chose to make. But, on this occasion, we were understaffed, and I was highly pressured by Adrian Becker, who, like any other fastidious curator, wanted to resolve the question immediately. The picture was a vain bit of foolishness entitled "Homage to the Square: Silent Hall" by the German-born Albers.

As our assistants carefully packaged the picture, I grew bored and vanished down the dim, deserted corridors of the silent museum, through the eerie hush that only the night can bring. I moved past the Futurists, Léger, all the Cubists, and the "School of Paris," and somehow, something seemed quite wrong—something was not quite right. And this peculiar feeling went far beyond my own particular doubts about the true status of these pictures, and even beyond my innate animosity towards the hubris of the entire establishment. There was something else wrong, something deeper, and I assumed it was my own present and personal isolation, and all these recurring uncertainties about my purpose and future. As I walked through the silence, I grew quite lonely, retraced my steps, and was grateful to find my associates. There was a certain comfort in watching these serious and conscientious men work so carefully and with such concern, even if it was only to protect and preserve an absurd blue canvas of redundantly overlapping squares. Later, out into the night at Fifty-Third Street, my uneasiness returned, and I even remember considering the unlikely possibility that we were being watched by someone or something unseen.

Hours later, deep in the night, I sat alone in a booth at Clancy's and watched the ice slowly melting within its bourbon as I considered the depth and pervasiveness of my loneliness. I'd met Jean Colfax at Oberlin in the Art School, but our natural attractions and sympathies slowly fell apart as she grew more modern, contemporary, and self-conscious. After graduation, we went to Boston together where I worked at the research lab of the Boston Museum of Fine Arts, and where Jean took a loft, painted little, and socialized most of her time. Soon she was gone for Paris, and her last card was brief, chicly disjunctive, and signed "Jeanette." But deep within myself, I was certain that our failing relationship was not really my most fundamental problem; for though I am convinced that a life without the mutual love and commitment of a woman is a shallow facade, my present problems were more those of the uncertain young man who finds himself inexorably moving from a salutary and constructive skepticism into a dark and dangerous and isolated cynicism.

Recently, I'd decided to cancel my summer lectures at NYU for the very reason that I'd, in a sense, chosen to give up trying to do those things which I'd previously felt were necessary and right. I'd come to feel that if I was to achieve nothing but abuse and disinterest for my honest questionings of the values and motives of most modern art, and if no one really cared about my estimations of the "passé" aesthetics and arts of the eighteenth century, then I'd gradually begun to find myself losing the necessary desire to confront the opposition. Sometimes, I would even find myself wondering if, in some way, I'd consciously chosen isolation and polemic not because of conviction but because of some deep personal failing. Although it was something that I never truly believed, the thought itself was indicative of my overall disillusionment.

Thinking back over the past few years, the best times were, strangely enough, those in Boston after Jean had left for Paris. I'd always had more of an impulse towards the scholarship than the artistic expression, and I was quite content to pursue my studies of Reynolds, and to use my not negligible creative talents in the judicious restoration of the old Masters at the Fine Arts Lab. But those times were made especially exciting because of my friendship with Jack Sinclair and his small circle of friends—with whom I shared the most outrageously unfashionable opinions, and from whom I learned all the essentials of my trade.

Jack was the absolute master of the process of authentication. His powers of stylistic observation were unparalleled, as was his ease of historical research and his unerring scientific analysis. Though still a young man, he'd already studied in the prestigious labs at Berlin and the British Museum, and he was now more than willing to teach me every meticulous aspect of the process: brushstrokes, carbon-14, micro-projection, spectroscopy, x-rays, infrared and ultraviolet, electron microbeam probes, crackle, varnishes, underpainting, and all the rest. However dull such terminology might sound, those were truly exciting times, full of productive and intriguing investigation, intense and meaningful discussion, and close fellowship with Jack and his circle. But when Jack suddenly left, the group quickly fell apart, the town's natural dullness asserted itself, and the work grew methodical. So I left as well. I went to NYU and began to suffer those, I suppose, inevitable insecurities and doubts of a young man, isolated and lonely, making a very unsure progress through his middle twenties.

Eventually, these fruitless recollections wore me down, and it was now quite late into the night. I left my drink, moved into the darks of the awesome New York City nightstreets, and walked through a fine light rain that was leaving a sharp wet sheen over the surface of the black streets, which then reflected the multifarious nightlights of the vibrant and central city of the declining West.

As the rain, so softly, wet my face as I moved through it, I was able to forget, for a time, my own confusions, and to recall the strange behavior of that young girl who had felt it necessary to slash that "Suprematist" picture because she felt its repulsiveness so indicative of the degeneration and decadence that proliferates and rises around us. And I wondered if, by now, she might have found a healthy means to vent or assuage her outrage, and I wondered if, at that very moment, she might be somewhere gently asleep within the soft comforting night of the skyscraper city.

Finally, arriving at Eighteenth Street, I quietly made my way upstairs. Despite these rather sympathetic thoughts, I still remained consciously uneasy about the entire evening, and I was actually quite unsurprised to find that a white folded note had been placed under the front door of my apartment. I lifted up the note and opened it in the soft yellow lights of the hallway. It was unaddressed, undated, and unsigned, and it contained only one word, written in a small but confident and striking script: "Disumbrationism."

★ ★ ★

OVER THE NEXT TWO WEEKS, we authenticated Albers' "Silent Hall." Although the tests were routine and conclusive, I often sat in on the verifications because I still had an uneasy feeling that something wasn't quite right. And no matter how much I reassured myself that it was probably just the effect of the message left under my door, the picture still seemed "wrong" in some indefinable way, and I was unable to ignore the dark, ominous, yet unclear repercussions of the telling word, "Disumbrationism."

The story behind that word is public record, and it even occurs as a reference in Upton Sinclair's *Mammonart*. In 1924, author Paul Jordan-Smith, fed up with what he felt were the talentless pretensions of modern art, took an old canvas and painted a most primitive and ludicrous figure: "an asymmetrical savage holding up what was intended to be a starfish." Jordan-Smith had never painted before and had only undertaken this exercise for the amusement of his immediate family. But when a local art critic admired the picture, Jordan-Smith, convinced that "the critics would praise anything unintelligible," entered the canvas—now called "Exaltation" and purportedly the work of "Pavel Jerdanowitch"—in a Chicago art exhibit in the spring of 1925. On April 6th, Comte Chabrier saw and reported the painting to the *Revue du Vrai et du Beau* in Paris, and soon the journal was contacting "Jerdanowitch" for biographical information.

Jordan-Smith wrote back that he was born in Moscow, had emigrated with his parents, lived in Chicago, grew tubercular, and went to the South Seas. He then returned to the United States and developed a new school and theory of painting called "Disumbrationism." In a very short time, Jerdanowitch's work was in high demand, and Jordan-Smith slapped off several more equally worthless pictures. Jerdanowitch's theories and work were now being discussed in *La Revue Moderne, Les Artistes d'Aujourd'hui,* and other contemporary periodicals, and when the new paintings were exhibited in Chicago at the Marshall Field galleries in 1926, his picture "Aspiration" was the only one of the four hundred pictures exhibited to be reproduced in *Art World.* The fraudulent painting received the highest praise and was described by one enthusiastic critic as "a delightful jumble of Gauguin, Pop Hart and Negro minstrelsy, with a lot of Jerdanowitch individuality."

In 1927, after a successful exhibit in New York City at the Waldorf, Jordan-Smith tired of the hoax and broke the story to the *Los Angeles Times.* The news quickly carried all over the world, but it was just as quickly forgotten by the art establishment, being yet another of those countless, successful, and most irritating hoaxes that had plagued modern art from its inception. In reflecting upon Jordan-Smith's curious story, it always seems especially important to give serious consideration to the possibility that if Jordan-Smith had not chosen to go public with the truth, his Disumbrationist works might now be hanging in revered sections of the Museum of Modern Art.

With this in mind, it was obvious to me that a hoax of some kind was presently being perpetrated at the Modern—or had already been perpetrated—and I grew more and more convinced that I was the intended victim. This might seem an undue self-absorption, but it was clear that something was wrong in all this, and that I was, at present, in the most vulnerable position. Nevertheless, I retained a confidence in my own professionalism and that of the Foundation's lab, and, despite certain misgivings, I decided to go, in person, to Becker's office at the museum to report our conclusions. It was a late but bright morning, and the sharp sunlight struck harsh and hurtful into my eyes, as it also gave to the Empire City that unreal effect when the sun's hyper-white lights illogically blur and confuse one's very perceptions.

When I found his door left open, I walked into the bright, cluttered, but empty room. Waiting, and looking over his desk, I noticed an envelope addressed to "A. Becker, Curator" on which the single word "Disumbrationism" appeared in the upper-left-hand corner. Quite impulsively, I took up the envelope, removed the note, and read the unsigned contents—written in the same, small, but strikingly familiar script:

> Kenneth Preston is very good, but he'll misread the truth. It matters little. It's but one of thirty hanging pictures which are copies—frauds of frauds—and rest

assured that I can make this revelation to the public at
any time. I know, very well, what I'm doing.

I was stunned.

I stood in shock, immobile, in the midst of the disheveled room
littered with the bright books, and journals, and reproductions
that all found their reflective share in the too-bright sunlight. The
enormity of the note's suggestion was so overwhelming—so utterly
audacious—that my own involvement and possible failings now
seemed of small consequence. Was it possible to walk down the
corridors of one of the most famous galleries in the world and be
surrounded by thirty fakes? I glanced off into the shafts of sunlight
that fell so sharply over the room from its high French windows,
and, somehow, I regained my composure. I replaced the note exactly,
left the room, and then walked down the hallway and waited.

Eventually, two quite agitated and preoccupied men approached
me from the far end of the corridor. When Becker saw me, though
clearly irritated by the timing of my intrusion, he was typically
cordial, even overly gracious.

"Preston, how are you?"

I stepped in their direction.

"Could you come inside?"

So I followed Becker and his associate back into his office.
The curator walked up to the front of his desk; then he turned
around to face me. I already knew at that point everything that
I cared to know, but I decided to stay. It was perfectly apparent
that fear and not the truth was the present necessity. I could tell
immediately that not only did Becker actually believe the note,
but that he'd already determined to do nothing about it.

"This is David Sloan."

I shook the stranger's hand. He was a wary, rather uncommunicative man in his mid-fifties who, it seemed to me, might know a great deal about life on the city streets outside but precious little about the pictures that hung in the other parts of this building. After an awkward silence, I could feel Becker's almost desperate wish to get rid of me. Finally, he got to the point.

"Any trouble with the Albers?"

"None. It's the one."

Despite his best efforts at self-control, Becker exuded an expression of unmitigated relief. But it was not the relief of a man who now had some reason to believe that the buried note on his desk might be incorrect; it was rather the relief of a man who was greatly comforted by the fact that I had been successfully duped by the author of that note.

There was another silence, and I'd had enough.

"I've got an appointment downtown."

There was further relief.

As I walked to the office door, I turned back.

"Any others?"

Becker looked me over with a very sharp and suspicious intensity, then he quickly regained his composure and spoke, as if in humor:

"Let's hope not, Kenneth."

The next day, I stayed alone in my room and tried to fathom the meanings and possibilities of the whole bizarre and unbelievable enterprise. David Sloan, as I'd suspected, was a private detective, and the very fact that Becker had failed to introduce Sloan under a false name indicated the curator's confusion, his preoccupation, and, most important, his conviction that the contents of the note were, no matter how incredible it might seem, the actual truth. So I pulled the window shades down, sat in the darkness of my apartment, and wondered if I too could believe that such a thing might be possible: that someone could actually fake thirty hanging pictures, and that anyone anywhere could pass a phony Albers past the scrutiny of the Foundation lab.

I knew, all too well, that the history of the pictorial arts was proliferate with fraud and forgery. In the ancient world, fake Grecian artifacts flooded into Rome, and even within the Western Renaissance, counterfeit works abounded—at one time, even Michelangelo agreed to carve a fraudulent piece so that Lorenzo de' Medici could hoax Cardinal Riario. The following century was duped by the countless frauds of Pietro della Vecchia and Luca Giordano. In the seventeenth century, Rubens (and later Ingres, Corot, and others) further complicated questions of authenticity by signing the work of his assistants. In more modern times, Millet's work had the distinction of being forged by the artist's own grandson, and the spurious Van Goghs of Otto Wacker earned him both large profits and eventual imprisonment. During the 1940s, the Dutch master-forger, van Meegeren, earned two million dollars selling his counterfeit Vermeers.

During his trial, aware of the increasing sophistication of scientific analysis, van Meegeren claimed, "It will never be possible to get away with forgery again." But he meant, of course, forging the Masters. For in the art of the present century, as contemporary critic George Savage has written, "The element of craftsmanship, essential to the detection of forgeries, seldom exists." And given that the market prices were so high, counterfeits of the moderns proliferated. The Hungarian Elmyr de Hory grew wealthy doing Dufy, Chagall, Léger, and countless others; Jean-Pierre Schecroun did Kandinsky, Braque, and Miró; untrained David Stein took a short prison term for his numerous Braques, Mirós, and Picassos; and Lothar Malskat served time for doing Klee, Utrillo, Picasso, and seventy other artists. One of the most intriguing and pertinent of the countless forgeries of modern art is the story of Jupp Jennicks, a simple-minded Cologne museum attendant (Porter at the Cologne Art Club in Hahner Gate) who did nineteen successful forgeries of Klee and Nolde without any previous training.

But individual buyers were not the only ones who succumbed to false work and unscrupulous dealers. The National Gallery in London admitted a false Francia in 1955, the Old Pinakothek took down a Goya in 1958, and the Vatican removed a Murillo in the following year. The list is quite endless, and the eerie and shady histories of certain smaller museums such as the Phoenix Art Museum, the Walker Art Center in Minneapolis, the Bass Museum of Art in Miami Beach, and the Chrysler Museum at Norfolk all serve as strident warnings that contemporary curators can be as fallible and gullible as individual buyers.

Nevertheless, however long I would consider the past and present histories of spurious work, credulous buyers, and museums with hanging frauds, still nothing could quite match the audacity of the present possibility. Sometimes, as I deliberated over this incredible scenario, I would, ironically, wonder if even Jack Sinclair could have seen through all the confusions and eventually comprehended whatever the truth might be. Then, remarkably, two days later, Jack Sinclair was dead. It was the first time that I'd actually heard about Jack since he'd vanished five years earlier, and the brief notice in the *Times* said that he'd "apparently been killed by street assassins." It also mentioned that he was employed as a "security guard at the Museum of Modern Art" and that he was survived by his wife, "Charlotte." Although certain things probably should have become quite clear, I actually felt nothing but grief and confusion as I drove out to Queens, that same evening, to attend the wake.

Jack and I had always had a great deal in common. We both came from families deeply interested in the pictorial arts: my father was a curator of a small museum in Ohio, and Jack's parents were well-to-do trustees at the Art Institute in Chicago. We both preferred the traditional Masters, and, where I specialized in the noble but enchanting lights and shadows of British Portraiture, Jack preferred the Renaissance and especially the delicate palette and poetic piety of Lippi's later work. He once said of "Madonna Adoring the Child in the Woods"—first done for the chapel in the Medici Palace and now at the Staatliche in Berlin—that it "instructed a hard and callous world to a soft beauty, a tenderness, and an inexplicable grace." But Jack's knowledge of the entire sweep of art history was encyclopedic, including the Moderns whom he detested as frauds, and his outspokenness on that particular subject and his conviction that a "willful moral abnegation" always underlies the "modernistic pretension" often caused him to be excluded and abjured by those with a personal and/or professional stake in the "integrity" of the modern enterprise.

Yet whatever we might have had in common, there was a crucial difference between us. I had accepted the fact that, creatively, I was talented without genius, and, in recognizing my abilities as well as my limitations, I was initially able to enjoy my artistic work despite its unfashionability by focusing on the scholarship. But Jack believed, quite sincerely, that he was gifted far beyond his contemporaries, and that only the currency of the times prevented his masterfully dramatic pieces from their properly deserved recognition. I had no doubt that this was true, and I spent much of our time together speaking of "patience," the justice of time, and "inevitability." But Jack was seven years older than I, and his patience was gone. Despite all his intellectual bravado, he was actually an extremely sensitive young man, and when his pictures were again rejected for exhibition in the "Contemporary Show" at the Boston Museum, it was not a great surprise to any of us that he finally decided to leave town—although the fact that he subsequently covered his tracks and dropped from sight was tragic for all his friends, and, now, of course, it clearly seemed a grim foreboding.

I walked into the funeral parlor and was directed into a quiet, dark, and somber room that I suppose was actually as comfortable as its purpose might allow. I looked over at the coffin, hesitated, and held out the hope for myself and everyone else that God might find a way to forgive us our constant trespass. Then I walked across the room and watched her closely as her face rose to mine. She had, I felt certain, been waiting for me, and as I stood above her, I recognized that the depths of her sufferings were somehow mercifully mitigated by the sense that something tragic, something uncontrollably tragic, was now, at long last, over. I wished again that I could help this young girl, that I might comfort her in her sorrow.

She remained seated and calm.

Then she spoke softly:

"Do you know who I am?"

"I believe I do."

"You once helped me amend a foolish act."

"I wish I could have done more."

I could tell by her reaction that she'd received the letter I'd written her two years ago after the slashing incident.

She grew thoughtful.

"I wasn't ready then."

This made me somewhat uncomfortable so I tried to say what I'd come to say.

"Jack was my closest friend."

When I hesitated, she took the moment to resolve an obvious misunderstanding.

"Kenneth, I'm his sister. Not his wife. The papers were incorrect."

With a suddenness that was almost frightening, everything changed. Everything now appeared in a new yet still unclear light. I was unsure how to react, but I managed to speak:

"Can we meet next week?"

"Yes."

Then, as I began to leave, she asked:

"Do you understand what's happened?"

"I think so . . . most of it."

It seemed she assumed as much. I looked at her once more before I left, and I saw in her face a most remarkable compassion, an understanding achieved through time and suffering, and a remarkable beauty.

★ ★ ★

SHE HAD ONCE SAID, "They've abandoned all care for the beautiful." And this was, of course, true, but they've abandoned far more than the beauty, having stripped from the arts the very values that made it fundamentally significant and worthy of esteem. They've forgotten that the artist must first be erudite and wise: that he must have the extensive liberal education that Da Vinci demanded, the understanding of human nature that

Aristotle demanded, and the earned wisdom *(sapere)* that Horace demanded. Similarly they've forgotten the necessary respect for the uniqueness of all true artistic talents and the necessity of hard-earned skills, apprenticeship, and craftsmanship, which all the pre-Croce aestheticians took as a given. Then, naturally, within their works themselves, they've chosen to ignore the most fundamental fact of all artistic expression—aspiration—and have concerned themselves only with their own self-indulgent, petty, and repulsive self-exposure. They've willfully ignored the Platonic insistence on man's transcendent urges: what the *Poetics* calls the "elevation of the soul"; Longinus, the "sublime"; Aquinas, "claritas"; and the early Enlightenment, the "ideal imitation."

To deny aspiration is not only to deny the divine, it is also to deny the natural world and the very essence of humanity. Da Vinci wisely called the arts "the grandchildren of nature and related to God"; so when they chose to deny aspiration and dehumanize art, they fell prey to the greatest possible crime—that of ignoring Plato's moral admonitions. It's one thing to fail in art, but it's quite another to damage the ethical sensibility of all those around us. It's the consummate, damning hubris of the current and fashionable relativist times to abjure these uncomfortable Platonic prescriptions about the inherent potential dangers of art, to disregard Pythagoras' conviction that music can and does influence character, and to ignore the Stoics' belief that the arts must have a moral efficacy. So the twentieth-century artist finds himself uneducated and unskilled but dangerously self-obsessed; he chooses to abandon standards and responsibilities, and then searches for his shallow "truth" within his own perverted self, thus abandoning all care for the beautiful.

If Croce and Breton can so easily convince themselves that all men have the capacity to create art, if Freud allows that art is merely the self-expression of neurosis, if Read elevates the primitive while emphasizing the abstract, and if Bell can insist that the "human" element must be expunged and that art is nothing but "form," then small wonder that the galleries are filled with self-indulgent exercises in pretension. Small wonder that Picasso in 1932 could so casually claim that the artist doesn't know in advance what he's about to paint—that he paints in a trance—unconscious, involuntary, and purely instinctive. Small wonder that an abused and rejected supremely talented young man, whose only sin was to reject the easy and fashionable currents of his times, might succumb to those formidable pressures, lose his sense of reality and propriety, and abandon his work for the single and solitary purpose of embarrassing and hoaxing what he saw as the bastion of all this mendacity. Small wonder that he would then dedicate five full years of his life to the insane and, in the end, perfectly worthless obsession of making absolutely perfect fakes of pictures he believed to be absolutely fraudulent.

So I spent much of the following week thinking over the tragedy and senselessness of it all, wondering from time to time exactly how he did it, and spending the rest of my time wondering how I should deal with Adrian Becker. In my subsequent rage and frustrations, I grew convinced that Becker had played a crucial part in Jack's death, and when I spotted a small notice in the *Times* that David Sloan had been temporarily retained by the Modern to "supplement its security force" in the wake of a rash of local burglaries, I was hardly dissuaded. But I was also painfully aware that I had absolutely no evidence, and that, in the most ironic and exasperating way, I was, due to my conclusions about the Albers, an unwitting affirmation that the only alleged forgery in the Modern was truly authentic. So I waited out the week, restraining my foolish impulses to confront Becker directly, and looking forward to my meeting with Charlotte.

As I walked past the lush green lawns of Central Park, within the shade of its majestic oaks, I could see her standing and waiting on the distant Gapstow Bridge, once again carefully dressed in her lovely white dress with its faint blue trim. Her beauty was so striking amid these serene surroundings that I suddenly hesitated and watched her from a distance. Eventually, I walked over to the bridge, and, as she told me the tragic story of her brother's deterioration, we wandered slowly and aimlessly around the park in the comforting shadows and soft lights of the sun.

Within four months of leaving Boston, Jack had effected the crucial step in his obsessive plan by securing employment as a security guard at the Museum of Modern Art. He'd forged his papers and employment history and willingly accepted work on the night shift. Charlotte told me that even before he'd left Boston, he'd already passed over forty spurious modern pastiches onto the market, and, once he was settled in New York, he immediately turned his profits to the procurement of materials, chemicals, and even a specially designed heating oven to effectively dry the oils.

Over the course of the next four years, late into the darkest evenings while the city slept around him, he laboriously created exact and perfect copies of those pictures which he particularly detested. His talents as an artist, his knowledge as a scholar, and his experience as a master restorer had made him, as he certainly well knew, the most impeccable and undetectable forger in art history. No photographs, no tests, and no analysis could, as I would eventually learn, catch his work. As time went on, his confidence and intensity increased, but his mental and emotional condition correspondingly deteriorated. By the time his sister Charlotte had finally found him, just two months ago, he seemed fully out of his mind with hatred—seething with vitriol. Fully understanding his confusions and rage, she found that she was able to mitigate his deepening despair, but she was unable to prevent his threatening notes to Becker, and, apparently, his warning to me.

As for his death, when I told Charlotte my convictions about Becker's involvement, she listened carefully and sympathetically, but she remained convinced that my suspicions were mistaken. She explained that Jack had recently had trouble on several occasions with night-roaming, inner-city street-gangs, and he'd willfully exacerbated their viciousness by taunting them with an unstable bravado. Charlotte was convinced that they'd finally caught up with him, and then beaten him beyond the threshold of his already weakened condition.

We spoke for hours.

I suppose we were able to expiate some of our sorrows, and I also suppose we were making the attempt to establish a friendship that might also be love. Yet, relentlessly, one crucial underlying question still haunted me about Jack and his whole forgery enterprise. Finally, as the evening came on, we passed the edge of a darkening pond, and I asked her directly.

"Are you certain that he *really* did it?"

"Yes."

I waited for more.

"He told me that he'd burned most of the originals in the Modern's furnaces on the same night that he finished his own copy and made the switch. But two of the canvases he'd rolled up and brought home. He kept them right under his bed as a kind of proof."

"You saw them?"

"I did, but before I could decide what to do, they vanished. That was about three weeks ago, and I'm not sure what he did with them."

As I wondered whether I should ask, she told me.

"One was 'Ma Jolie.' The other was 'The Mocker Mocked.'"

If I could have found something to smile about in this whole tragic affair, it could only have been the thought of Jack's secret and unqualified delight in making those two particular choices. Then I wondered out loud:

"How did he plan to prove it?"

"I don't know. I never asked."

Charlotte grew pensive, and I considered the probability that whatever Jack might have done to "mark" the forgeries to prove his authorship, it might never be discovered.

Then she remarked, rather reflectively:

"I suppose it really doesn't matter."

Here was a young woman who'd been so distraught by the assumptions of modern art that she'd, just two years earlier, quit her position as an art teacher in the Westchester school system, found her confused way to the Modern Art, and violently slashed open one of its permanent collection. But she'd eventually come to believe that you can't really "destroy" modern art, and she'd learned from Jack's tragedy that, no matter what he might have done, it's always senseless and self-destructive to waste time trying to hoax it. And *I* was now learning, very slowly, but with a growing certainty, that it's just as foolish to turn away and attempt to ignore it. We'd all been wrong. When one is faced with what one feels to be an entrenched, dishonest, and hostile opposition, one is obliged not to strike back blindly but to make an honest attempt to illuminate, and thus, hopefully, expose the infectious error. One must hold one's ground, reveal the truth, and let time have its curative way.

Within a few months, I would reschedule my lectures at NYU, and Charlotte would resume her teaching. We would find in the ashes of our previous personal despair a love and aspiration and re-dedication. And sometimes, whenever things might look temporarily bleak and disheartening, we would visit the inspiring collection at the Metropolitan, or fly to Florence or Amsterdam or Rome or London. And, sometimes, we would even walk, once again, down those uneasy corridors of the Modern, and, holding hands, we'd once again challenge, but without a blind vindictiveness, the very motives and effects of all those grotesque and disinterested canvases surrounding us—all the time wondering, I'm sure, though it didn't really matter, which ones of these pictures were merely frauds, and which ones were frauds of frauds.

Screwball

The Energetics of a Thrown Ball: we find that the throw takes about 0.11 seconds and that the average force on the ball of about 12 pounds generates a mean acceleration of the ball of about 40 g's—forty times the acceleration of gravity.

— Robert K. Adair, *The Physics of Baseball*

IT WAS THE FOURTH AND FINAL GAME of the World Series: Ricky Kight, with the look of a hired 6'4" gunslinger, had walked in from the bullpen with a 1-0 lead in the eighth and struck out the side. Then he whiffed Gonzales to start off the bottom of the ninth, got Marshall on a broken-bat blooper to short left, and was now facing down Ramirez with a 2-2 count.

"Will he send," one of the announcers wondered rhetorically, "the juice, the split curve, or his nasty screwgie?"

Every baseball fan in America, of course, was wondering exactly the same thing as Ricky took the sign, went into his windup, and then, with that peculiar, idiosyncratic, and inexplicably odd arm motion, threw what Mathewson used to call a "fadeaway," and what Carl Hubbell later called a "screwball," and what the umpire called a "strike!" It was over. The Yankees had swept the World Series for the ninth time. The stadium erupted, the players went nuts, and Keith hit the pause button on his laptop.

That was eight months ago, when Ricky Kight, who was Keith's old high school friend and teammate, had capped off an absolutely unprecedented season (19-0, 1.34 ERA) with an absolutely unprecedented World Series: winning a first-game shutout and then closing down the last three games with an efficiency and intimidation that reminded everyone in America of Mariano Rivera at his best. Then, a month later, his career was suddenly over. He was helping a friend move a piano, smashed his right shoulder, and damaged his rotator cuff (not irreparably), his scapular, his tendons, his muscles, and, far more severely, his radial nerve. At first, given the "piano" aspect of the story, it almost seemed like a joke, or a hoax, and it got lots of clever headlines in the *Post* and all over the web, but it was definitely no joke, and even Ricky's always-optimistic high-powered sports agent, Mike Rodgers, had eventually accepted and announced the terminality of the fact at a tumultuous press conference with a kind of stunned disbelieving bemusement.

But now, *even that,* even the shocking career-ending injury seemed like just another biographical quirk, just another strange baseball-history anecdote or footnote, because Ricky was dead, dying in a head-on just two months ago after a charity event in Atlantic City, having stopped off at Barnegat Light on the way home to Morristown, to stare at the ocean, which had always given him a sense of inexplicable serenity, before getting himself smacked by some forty-year-old unemployed drunk driver (0.33 blood/alcohol level) on Long Beach Boulevard.

Keith sat in his spotless uniform in his spotless cruiser, no longer staring at the screen on his laptop, but staring at the great gray Lady in the Harbor, two thousand feet away, in New Jersey waters, in the upper Hudson Harbor, which always induced in him a sense of inexplicable serenity. He sat silently in patrol car #257 at the southeast "overlook" extremity of Liberty State Park, not far from the picnic area, not far from US Flag Plaza, watching one of the Circle Line Ferries from the CRRNJ Terminal glide over the bluish waters, south of Ellis Island, and heading for Liberty Island and the Statue of Liberty. Keith always loved this place, and he loved the New York Harbor, and he loved the Lady, and he loved New Jersey.

Then Keith looked back at his screen, hit a few keys, and stared again at Ellen's typically straight-to-the-point e-mail:

> Elizabeth Kight called. She'll be stopping at East District
> HQ around 5:15.

Naturally, as a result, Keith had the Kights on his mind. Thinking about Ricky, and the night they beat Ocean Township and won the Group III State Championship in their senior year with Ricky's impeccable three-hitter. Thinking about standing there, uselessly, holding down the line at third base, watching Ricky mow them down, one after another, alternating his I-didn't-even-see-the-damn-thing fastball with his already big-league split-finger. Thinking also about later that night, celebrating with the guys, drunk out of his mind and watching Ricky, always thoughtful, always likeable, always sober, yet still enjoying himself in the midst of all the raucousness. Thinking also, of course, about Lizzie, whom he'd been chasing since they were kids, with whom he'd gone to his junior and senior proms, to whom he proposed to three years ago, who'd said "no" because he was too immature, which was true.

Two hours later he was sitting in the Lieutenant's office. Waiting.

"Can I borrow your office for a half-hour after you go home tonight?" he'd just asked, getting one of those convince-me-more looks from the Lieutenant who liked Keith a lot but didn't want to create some kind of awkward precedent.

"My old girlfriend's coming by," Keith explained with some effect. But not enough, so he kept it rolling:

"I proposed to her three years ago, and she said no."

"Why?"

"She said I was too immature and stupid, and then she proved it."

"How?"

"She said, 'You've been playing baseball your whole life and I bet you don't even know how many stitches there are on a baseball."

"Did you know?"

"No."

The boss thought it over for a minute.

"Has she married anyone else in the meantime?"

"No."

So Keith got the nod, and now he was sitting alone in the office of Lieutenant Jack Butler, in a room so neat and efficient it could, in its own way, serve as a warning and even an explanation to anybody in Jersey City with bad intentions, with some kind of criminal impulse, about why it was a bad idea to proceed, and even about why the department's arrest-and-conviction rate was so high and efficient, especially here in the East District. Then Lizzie walked into the room wearing a lovely white summer dress, and Keith stood up. He remembered, not that his mind needed much prodding, why he'd always felt about her the way he did, and still did.

Lizzie smiled.

"You look good in that uniform," she said.

"You look much better than good," he said rather stupidly.

So they sat down, and they talked briefly about the catch-up stuff they didn't get a chance to discuss at the funeral because she was too damaged and too devastated. So they talked briefly about *him*—about his recent commendation, and his night classes at John Jay in Criminal Justice, and his inexorable progress along the department's detective track—and they talked briefly about *her*—about her studies at Columbia, and her new apartment on Morningside Heights, and her recent decision to go into estates and wills, "so I can try to help some people out." But in the midst of all the "catching up," it was clear to the both of them that what they *really* needed to talk about was Ricky, which was why she was here.

Finally, when they got around to it, Lizzie was pretty blunt.

"I'd like you to look into it, Keith," she said. "I know I can trust you to tell me the truth."

But Keith was more than a little bit baffled since Ricky's crash in North Beach seemed like it was pretty much cut-and-dry. Of course, there were, naturally, those unconscionable Internet rumors that Ricky had become depressed after wrecking his arm with the piano, and that he was hooked on prescriptions, and that he was even suicidal, but Keith had never believed any of it, so he asked Lizzie what she *really* meant:

"The truth about what?"

"About the last three years," she said, as if not really certain herself what she was looking for. "About that shoulder accident," she continued. "Something wasn't right. And about what *really* happened after our mom died and after Ricky quit the Indians."

The "official" MLB narrative on Ricky had gone something like this: after graduating from Morristown High School, Ricky had been signed by the Cleveland Indians, and he'd kicked around the minor leagues for about two-and-a-half years, beginning with the Kinston Indians in North Carolina, moving up to the Akron Aeros, and then pitching for the triple-A Columbus Clippers before being called up to the Indians as a closer. But Ricky had been less-than-mediocre in his first crack at the bigs. His fast ball was definitely fast enough, but it had no hop, and he certainly couldn't make it on his split-finger alone. He saved three, blew four, and had a disastrous 5.67 ERA, so he quit the team before they had a chance to send him back down to the minors. Then, for the next two years, he essentially vanished, returning to New Jersey, hiring Pedro Velasquez as his personal pitching coach, and somehow finding more hop on his fastball and cultivating a devastatingly deceptive screwball.

The rest, of course, is Yankee lore: he finagled an invite to spring training in Tampa, walked onto Steinbrenner Field the day after Valentine's Day—just a year ago last February—and struck out the first sixteen batters he faced. By opening day, he was in the starting rotation, and long before the All-Star break, he was the ace of the staff. It was shades of Mark Fidrych and Vida Blue and Russ Ford, but the numbers were even better. Much better. The numbers were unbelievable. If he hadn't sprained his wrist and missed five starts in August, he might have ended up 24-0.

"So I guess you're not buying the standard bio?" Keith asked.

"I don't know what to believe," Lizzie admitted.

So Keith said yes.

It was a simple fact that Keith could never say no to Lizzie, and he had a few sick days coming, so he talked to the Lieutenant, and by the next afternoon, he was "on the case," although he had no idea what he was doing, sitting on the exterior patio of the University Hospital, staring at the Newark skyline, waiting for his one-time rival.

Dr. Alan Palmer, already a renowned orthopedic specialist in the metro area, had been Ricky's older friend and mentor in high school and his personal physician after Ricky left the Indians. The Kights and the Palmers, a family of distinguished physicians, had always been close personal friends, and they lived right next to each other on the same upscale block in Morristown. They were definitely a class or two above Keith's more middle-class background, but they were never really snobby about it. As for Alan, back in his high school days, about five years before Ricky and Keith, he'd pitched some pretty good numbers for the Morristown Colonials, and he was more than glad, years later, to help Ricky with his motion, his split-finger curve, and his training regimen. Then last November, he asked Ricky to help him move his piano.

"It was what it was," Alan shrugged, as if still amazed by what had happened. "It was just a terrible fluky accident. It damaged several nerves, but most specifically Ricky's radial, and that was that. Both his thumb and his forefinger went numb, and he lost his grip and some of his arm strength, and that was that."

"But don't nerves come back? Don't they regenerate?"

"Sure, sometimes," Alan nodded, "but not when the damage is that extensive. Besides, to be a major-league ballplayer these days, you can't pitch with anything less than one hundred percent nerve sensation."

Keith didn't doubt that it was true.

So they talked a bit more, and Alan was relaxed and certainly more than generous with his time, but Keith still didn't know what to think.

"Please give my best to Lizzie," Alan said as they shook hands.

"I will," Keith nodded. Then he watched as the doctor, who was recently married, walked away.

Later that same afternoon, Keith was sitting alone in the deserted grandstands at the Colonials' ball field. He hadn't been back since graduation when he'd gone off to the police academy and Ricky had gone off to play for the Kinston Indians in North Carolina. But it felt good, right now, to be back at Morristown High and to see the field in such a beautiful pristine condition. After all, what was more beautiful than a baseball diamond? It had always seemed to Keith—both in the abstract and in reality—that a baseball field, *any* baseball field, was like some mystical yet perfectly functional combination of an elysian field, a playground, and a battlefield, each combined together with the mathematical perfection and precision of a geometric equation.

Then, somewhat inexplicably, Keith remembered one time when they were little kids back at Assumption Grammar School when Ricky had turned to Keith and said, kiddingly:

"You know what the alien leader said to the alien spaceship captain, who was about to blast off for earth and asked, 'But how will I know which place is America?'?"

So Keith, maybe seven years old at the time, just shrugged and said, "What?"

"Look for the beautiful diamonds."

Which was true, and for the rest of his life, whenever Keith flew in a plane and there was visibility of the ground beneath him, he would find himself spotting and counting the innumerable baseball diamonds as he glided with pleasure through the lower atmosphere.

When his cell phone rang, it was the senior cop on the scene at Ricky's crash in North Beach. They talked a bit, and the cop confirmed that the accident was exactly what it seemed to be—some drunken moron had swerved into Ricky's lane and smacked him dead-on, and they were both dead instantly. There was nothing peculiar or suspicious about it. Sadly, it was rather routine. Keith thanked the cop for the callback, and he believed him implicitly. Then he checked his watch. It was time for the coach.

Coach Myers sat in his office looking almost exactly as he had four years ago, surrounded by his cluttered room—surrounded by trophies, and photos, and memorabilia, and his amazingly absurd collection of over three hundred baseball bobbleheads. When Keith walked in, Coach Myers stood up and they shook hands. The coach wasn't much of a "hugger"—and neither was Keith—but the old man's handshake was warmer than a million phony hugs. There was never any doubt that Coach Myers was "old school," and he'd always pushed his kids too hard, but they loved him anyway. Underneath the old "tough guy" from Morris Plains was a coach with a caring heart, not to mention a keenly analytical baseball mind.

So they talked about the "old days," and then they talked about the "new" days, but, soon enough, they went right back to the "old" days again. Coach Myers was obviously very proud of what Ricky had accomplished, but he was also completely baffled by his subsequent career and death.

"He was such a damned-good kid," he remembered, "a serious

church-going-book-reading kind of kid—not just another wiseass like you—and nobody ever worked harder."

But . . .

Although the coach never actually said the word "but," there was clearly some kind of unexpressed "but" going on, and Keith eventually got the old man to talk about it.

"I guess," he admitted, almost reluctantly, "that I never really believed the whole 'improvement' story."

Which seemed very peculiar, of course, since there was absolutely no doubt that during Ricky's two-year hiatus from the majors, he had, with his new pitching coach and his new training regiment, somehow drastically improved his pitching. Even improving it to legendary and record-setting proportions.

So Keith pressed harder.

"Look, Keith," the coach explained, "you can't put a hop in a fastball that isn't already there, and that screwy screwball seemed more a result of Ricky's new motion than some new grip or increased forearm pronation."

Then the coach flipped on his computer and called up a short film clip that he'd obviously watched several hundred times. It was from a home game last July at Yankee Stadium when the announcers were analyzing Ricky's motion and showing it in extreme slow motion.

"Look at that," Coach Myers said, as he and Keith stared at the large screen on the cluttered desk and watched, in super-slow motion, Ricky's undeniably peculiar, three-quarters sidearm, almost "herky-jerky" motion in both the acceleration phase and his follow-through.

Then they watched it several more times in silence.

"That's not what Ricky looked like when he pitched for me.

Do you remember any of that weirdo 'arm-snap' in his motion?"

"Not really, but I guess I was watching the hitters and not Ricky."

"Well, if I remember correctly," the coach kidded, "you were busy watching the girls in the stands, especially Ricky's little sister."

They both smiled and talked some more, and, except for their obvious concerns about Ricky, it was the best time Keith had had in years.

> *How to Throw a Screwball:* At the end of the release the pitcher must follow through in a similar fashion to finishing a curveball, except his hand will be moving down the left side of the ball. During this time, the forearm will also pronate, turning inward. ("What is a Screwball?" James Lincoln Ray)

Later the same day, in the falling twilight, Keith drove through Morristown, his hometown, which had once been Washington's headquarters during the winter of 1777 and also during the record-setting brutal winter of 1779, surrounded by his ragtag army, and Hamilton, and Lafayette, and even Benedict Arnold who was court-martialed on the Morristown Green. Just before cruising past the Green, Keith detoured near the old Schuyler-Hamilton House, where Hamilton had once courted and later proposed to Betsy Schuyler. Then he drove south into the upscale Historic District, cut over to Beacon Street, and pulled up a long tree-lined driveway to the Kight's old colonial, where he'd be spending the next few days. Lizzie had given him the house key at the precinct, along with complete access to all of Ricky's papers, his financial records, and his computer records.

"I trust you, Keith," she'd said when she gave him the key,

and he knew that she meant it.

Keith carried his bags inside, set up quickly in the guest room on the second floor, and looked out the window to the backyard where, three years earlier, he'd knelt down in front of Lizzie, beneath that red oak tree, and proposed.

Then he heard her say no.

Then he heard her give her reasons why.

For about three weeks before his rejected proposal, Keith had been mulling over the idea of trying to lure Lizzie over to Schuyler House since it had worked so well for Hamilton back in March 1780, but he'd finally decided that it would be best to ask her at her own home, which she loved so much. And even after his failure and the rejection, Keith knew, in his heart, that the problem wasn't the *place* of the proposal, it was the proposer.

Lizzie was right. He'd run through his adolescence with a loud and tough-guy crowd at Morristown High, and he still hadn't gotten it out of his system. Sure, he was a Jersey City rookie cop with a Glock 22 on his hip, but he was still a kid, and he knew it, and he knew that she was right. Besides, at the same time, she was also being pursued by Alan Palmer, who was already a hotshot doctor and just getting his ortho practice up-and-running in Newark. But Keith never believed that Lizzie had turned him down for Alan, and, whether she had or whether she hadn't, about a year later, she turned Alan down too, and when Keith finally asked Ricky about it, he'd just shrugged and said:

"I don't know, maybe she still has plans for you."

Which, back then, gave Keith hope—and which still gave him hope as he stared out the window of the home she'd grown up in.

Two days later, after endless hours of papers and folders and contracts and bank statements, Keith had gotten nowhere except frustrated. On his breaks, he'd been calling up lots of Ricky's old teammates and coaches and managers and associates, like Mike Rodgers, his agent; Pedro Velasquez, his pitching coach; and even Derek Jeter—who were all very willing to talk about Ricky, whom they all obviously liked, but none of them had been able to give Keith the slightest lead of any kind. Of course, part of the problem was that he didn't even know what he was looking for.

On his other breaks, Keith would munch on M&Ms and browse through an old cardboard box full of fan mail that Ricky kept in the corner of his bedroom. Most of Ricky's "routine" fan mail ("send me a photo," "send me an autograph," "send me an autographed photo") had been handled at the Yankees' front office, but Ricky had always done his best to read and respond to the more personal stuff, and, for whatever reason, he'd saved this pile right in his own bedroom. Most of the letters were from tragically sick kids, or from regular kids who'd been inspired by his hard work and amazing comeback, or from soldiers overseas, some in war zones, wishing him their best during his record-breaking season.

But there was another one, and it certainly wasn't a fan letter, and it came postmarked: "Lancaster, Kentucky."

> Dear Mr. Kight, I know exactly what you've done, and I can't tell you how disappointed I am. You will have to find your own way to live with the guilt and deal with your Maker and your own conscience. I only write this note to encourage you to let things go no farther. At the very least, the secret should be kept a secret.—Harvey Hopkins, Jr.

Keith immediately googled the man's name and read the brief Wikipedia entry:

> Harvey Hopkins (born Lancaster, Kentucky, August 13, 1934, died in Lancaster, Kentucky, July 5, 1952) was a legendary high school pitcher who pitched for the Lancaster High School "Green Devils" baseball team.
>
> Following a promising but unspectacular sophomore season (8-6), Hopkins was involved in a combine accident on his father's farm during the fall harvest at the beginning of his junior year and severely injured his right (pitching) arm. By his senior year, however, Hopkins had fully recuperated, winning every game he pitched (18-0), with a 1.11 ERA (still a Kentucky high school record), with 316 strikeouts (still the national single-season high school record). He had uncommon control, a moving fastball, a deceptive swooping curve, and a baffling screwball.
>
> After leading the Green Devils to the Division II Kentucky State Championship, he signed a letter of intent with the Cincinnati Reds, but the following summer, Hopkins died in a fluke accident while he was taking a swimming break from working on his father's farm on the day after Independence Day. Along with a few friends, he'd gone to Morgan's Quarry for a swim in the whirlpool when he slipped on the rocks and struck his head on the ground, smashing his right temple into a quarry stone and dying instantly at the age of eighteen.
>
> But Harvey Hopkins is still a legend in Kentucky sports history.

Keith read it again.

Then he called the airlines.

The next morning he flew into Kentucky's Blue Grass Airport (LEX), secured his Hertz rental car, and drove the twenty-seven miles from Lexington to Lancaster, all the time calling Harvey Hopkins, Jr., who was, apparently, the grandnephew of the long-dead pitching sensation. But no one would pick up the phone. Late last night, after midnight in Morristown, Keith had managed to track down Hopkins' e-mail address, and he'd sent him a message, and early this morning, right before his flight from Newark, he'd received a seven-word response:

I'm afraid I have nothing to say.

As Keith headed south on Route 27, he also called the Lancaster Police Department, but the chief of police was off at the Garrard County Fair, as were, apparently, many of the other cops on the local force. So Keith drove directly to the Ashley Inn, a restored Southern mansion bed-and-breakfast on Lexington Road, dropped off his bags, and headed out to the fairgrounds. Almost aimlessly, he wandered around the 4-H exhibits, the animal pens, the arts-and-crafts showcases, the cotton candy booths, and the outdoor amphitheater which was thumping with a bluegrass band. Every section of the fairgrounds seemed jammed with happy kids and with their not-so-unhappy parents, and Keith was able to talk with many of the locals and with some of the local on-duty cops. Fortunately, everyone seemed more than willing to talk about the legendary Harvey Hopkins, sometimes embellishing his already unembellishable statistics, and always assuring the "Yankee" from New Jersey that Harvey was just a good ol' boy, a real nice farm kid, who seemed to be just as astonished by his pitching good fortune and success as everyone else.

Then one of the old-timers, standing over by the quilts exhibition, added:

"It's just too bad about those bastards who messed with his grave."

Two other younger men agreed.

"Yeah, it sure bothered Harvey, Jr., a ton."

"Well, who could blame him?" the third man asked rhetorically.

"When did it happen?" Keith wondered.

"Oh, about three years ago," the old-timer remembered.

Eventually, Keith figured out that the chief of police wasn't at the fair on duty. He was there with his grandkids, and Keith finally tracked him down in the amusement park where the chief was watching two of his little granddaughters whipping around on a mini-rollercoaster. Keith showed the chief his Jersey City badge, and Chief Brodie, a pleasant but country-tough guy in his late fifties, seemed glad to talk.

"Well, it wasn't *just* a grave desecration," he explained, "it was much worse. They actually dug up the body."

Keith was amazed.

"I sure do wish I'd caught those bastards," he said, "but they came with a backhoe late one Sunday night and they probably finished everything in an hour or so. They even reburied the coffin, probably thinking that no one would notice, but Harvey, Jr., sure did, and we dug it up again."

"What did they want?"

"Souvenirs, I guess," the chief shrugged, with visible disgust and anger. "But what the hell could anyone do with 'souvenirs' like that?"

At that exact moment, Keith understood everything.

He nodded, almost reflexively, at the chief, and stared up at the Ferris wheel as it slowly turned against the deep blue Kentucky sky. He felt staggered by what he now knew. It hardly seemed possible. Then he turned back to the chief.

"They took the right arm, didn't they?"

"Yeah. Real sickos if you ask me."

When Keith got back to the Ashley Inn, the girl at the desk said he had a visitor waiting in the outside garden. It was Harvey Hopkins, Jr.

Hopkins was a quite good-looking, athletic guy in his late thirties or early forties, who, despite his pleasant demeanor, seemed a man burdened with worries. He explained that he'd changed his mind about meeting with Keith after sending his e-mail this morning, but he'd been gone to Lexington for most of the day with his six-year-old son. He apologized for his lack of "hospitality," and he explained his reasons, which Keith now fully understood.

"So Ricky flew down here after you sent him that letter?"

"That's right," Hopkins explained. "And I was surprised he came, and I was surprised by the kind of man he was. He was a regular decent guy, very sincere, and wracked with guilt. I actually ended up feeling sorry for him. It was hard to imagine how a nice guy like that could have gotten himself mixed up in something like this. At any rate, I guess the letter I sent really shook him up. He even asked me later if there was a Catholic priest in the area, and I sent him over to see Fr. Thomson on Prescott Street."

"Did Ricky know about the exhumation?" Keith asked.

"He did, but he thought it had been done legally—with the permission of the family—and he apologized. All he wanted to do was set things right, and all I wanted to do was keep the 'secret' secret and put old Harvey back together again."

Keith understood, and he nodded.

"And that's why," Hopkins explained further, "I'm meeting with you right now," and, once again, Keith understood perfectly, and he nodded.

About an hour later, Keith was sitting in the rectory of St. Andrew's Catholic Church with Fr. Thomson, a billion-year-old priest who seemed to be able to "read" people like Padre Pio used to do, but, for some reason, it didn't make Keith nervous.

"He wanted," the old priest explained, "to talk about the morality of what he called the 'unfair advantage.' His mother had died, and he'd lost his job, and he'd made some bad choices that had given him an 'unfair' or 'unnatural' advantage in his line of work. He was a bit vague about exactly what that was back then, which was fine, but I've been following the big leagues for over eighty years, and I'd seen him on TV, and I figured it out."

The priest looked directly at Keith.

"I guess you have too?"

"I guess I have."

"Well, don't be too hard on your old friend. You and I have made some stupid mistakes too."

Keith understood, and the old priest continued:

"All he wanted to do was make amends, and I believed him. I could tell he was a good man—a bit like the original Harvey Hopkins—and I liked that boy a lot too. I still keep him in my prayers."

The next morning, Keith was back in New Jersey, sitting right back in the empty stands at the Colonials' baseball field, the now-deserted scene of so many of Ricky's adolescent triumphs.

Eventually, Alan made his way up from the field, and he sat next to Keith, who wasted no time.

"I know what happened, Alan," Keith warned him, "I've been to Kentucky."

Alan didn't seem surprised; he didn't even seem that uncomfortable. He seemed like a man who was ready and willing to unburden himself and he did. He told Keith that he'd first heard about Harvey Hopkins, the Kentucky pitching legend, when he was still at Cornell Med School in Manhattan, when an older doctor, a diehard baseball fan as well as an orthopedic specialist, had told him about Harvey over a beer one night—and started speculating about the combine accident.

"Whatever he did to his arm in that accident, it must have created just the right kind of torque to make his pitches move and hop. Let's face it, no seventeen-year-old kid can throw a screwball without wrecking his arm unless his arm isn't like any other kid's arm."

The specialist continued:

"You know what, Alan? I'd love to know exactly where those breaks occurred. I'd love to get a good look at that kid's arm. From what I've read, he had breaks in all three bones: the humerus, several in the radius, but only one in the ulna."

Alan, of course, knew exactly what the never-named orthopedist was suggesting. If you knew exactly where the breaks were, and if you broke the arm of someone else in exactly the same places, then you might—although there were certainly no guarantees—just have another million-dollar arm.

"So when Ricky's career in Cleveland went south," Alan continued, "and his mom had died, and he couldn't accept that all his hard work wasn't enough to do what he wanted to do—and what he felt he was destined to do—we decided to try it. You've got to remember, Keith, that I was incredibly young and stupid and ambitious back then, and I was still obsessed with baseball. It was a hard thing to resist: Could I *really* make a pitcher's arm better with a not-that-complicated operation? Could I *really* help my best friend do what he wanted to do? Besides, back then, I foolishly thought that if I helped Ricky out, it might get me in better with Lizzie, but that was idiotic too, especially after the Hopkins family refused to allow me to examine the skeleton. So I broke the law, and I hired three guys to get it for me illegally."

"But how did you convince yourself to do it?" Keith wondered, not so much in a judging kind of way, but more in a concerned-and-disbelieving kind of way.

Alan shrugged.

"I guess I just rationalized everything away. I told myself that I was helping my friend, and that there was no real harm done in Kentucky. I told those guys to put the grave back exactly like they found it. No one was even supposed to know about it."

He paused a moment, then continued.

"At any rate, Ricky was never a part of that crap, and all the rest of it is pretty 'iffy' anyway."

"Iffy? What do you mean by that?"

"I guess I mean the ethics of it. Let's face it, is it *really* so wrong for an athlete to have an operation to enhance his performance? Athletes have operations all the time. Too many in fact."

"But they're repairing existing injuries," Keith said, "they're not mutilating themselves."

"I put six breaks in Ricky's right arm, and it was a fairly easy operation, and he recuperated quickly. He never *looked* mutilated and he never *felt* mutilated. Besides, actors have plastic surgery to enhance their careers, right? So why not athletes? And that's how I tried to rationalize everything back then, despite the utter stupidity of it all."

"And Ricky too?"

"Yeah, I guess so, but mostly he just put it out of his mind. You know how obsessed he could get with conditioning and training, and he seemed to take it like any another physical and mental challenge. He went about his usual life, working day and night to master that damned screwball, still seeing his old friends on occasion—like you—even going to church every day, and doing his best to ignore the conscience within. At least, until he received that letter from Lancaster."

Keith nodded.

"So the whole piano thing was a fake?"

"Yeah," Alan confirmed. "Once Ricky had decided that what he was doing was 'cheating,' he wanted no more of it, but he couldn't come clean about it at the time since he'd spoken with that nephew down in Kentucky, and they were determined to keep the 'secret' secret. If Ricky had quit the Yankees in mid-season and confessed everything, then down the road, other young kids and unethical doctors like me would also have attempted to restructure their pitching arms. Besides, he was concerned about me, given what I'd done in Kentucky."

"The legalities?"

"Sure, I could *still* lose my license. Besides, there were other problems too. Ricky had lots of charitable obligations last season that he didn't want to bail on, so he and Hopkins decided that he'd play out the season, do his best, and then find a way out of it in the off-season. Thus, the piano nonsense."

Even though Keith had already figured things out in that

single bizarre instant standing next to Chief Brodie at the Garrard County Fair, it was quite another thing to sit in the grandstands and listen to Alan describing the indescribable.

"And the 'sprained wrist'?" Keith finally asked.

"Yeah, that was just to limit his statistics," Alan explained. "Once Ricky was certain that the Yankees had the pennant sewed up, and that he wasn't letting his teammates down, he took off a few games. He didn't want to go 24-0."

So they sat in the silence for a few moments.

"It was like Frankenstein," Alan finally admitted, as if conjuring up some inexplicable bad dream that really wasn't a dream at all. "I'd become obsessed with the science of the thing— and with helping out Ricky—and I lost sight of everything around me. Even my future. I even desecrated a young man's grave. It's hard to believe."

Alan seemed truly stunned by what he'd done, and he was obviously full of self-disgust.

He also seemed honestly repentant.

"The best thing that ever happened to the both of us," Alan explained, "was that letter from Lancaster."

So they sat in the stands, in a much longer silence, just staring at the bright greens of the grass and the perfection of the baseball diamond.

Keith tried, as best he could, to be understanding. He was fully aware that when he was younger he would have done exactly the same thing—exactly what either one of them had done, the doctor or the baseball pitcher. He would have put on the blinders and rushed full steam ahead into an unpurgeable remorse and shame, and now, at this particular moment, sitting above his old high school baseball field, the very fact that he now realized this about himself and abhorred it, made him also realize that, like both Alan and Ricky, he'd also grown up a bit too.

"Where's the arm?"

"I sent it back to Kentucky."

> *The Acceleration Phase*: Once the arm reaches maximal external rotation, the elbow joint begins to extend, and the shoulder joint rapidly internally rotates and adducts, initiating the acceleration phase of throwing. The acceleration phase of the overhead throw has been reported to be the fastest human motion recorded. During the acceleration phase, the maximal internal rotation/adduction velocity exceeds 7000 degree/s. ("Physiology of Baseball," Kevin E. Wilk)

The next day Keith met with Lizzie in the backyard of her Morristown home, and he told her everything. Then he explained that Ricky was planning to slowly sink back into obscurity, doing whatever charity work he could off his dwindling fame. He was, according to what Alan had said, even thinking of going to college, and sometimes wondering about the seminary and about whether he might ever deserve such a thing. Naturally, Lizzie was both upset and relieved by all the revelations, but she was comforted by the fact that Ricky had been getting his life in order when that pathetic drunken driver had smashed the both of them to death at the New Jersey shore.

"Hopkins' little boy, Jackie, has leukemia," Keith pointed out, "but he's making progress at the Cancer Center at the University of Kentucky."

"Which explains that donation Ricky made last summer," Lizzie remembered, now fully understanding.

"Yeah," Keith agreed, "and I think he intended it to be the first of many."

There was, for a moment, some hesitation beneath the red oak tree.

"He was making amends, Lizzie," Keith assured her, "in the best ways he could."

Lizzie nodded, and she seemed reassured, and, eventually, Keith felt the time was right to change the subject.

"You know," he said with a smile, "this is right where somebody proposed to somebody else three years ago."

Lizzie smiled as well.

"So what?" she kidded. "Are you planning to try again?"

"Not yet."

Lizzie smiled at that too.

"But I've got two tickets for the Yankee game Wednesday night," he said.

"But you're a Mets fan!" she said with mock disdain.

"Well, they're playing the Mets," Keith explained. "It's an interleague game, so we can root against each other."

Lizzie didn't say yes, but Keith knew by her particular silence and by her particular demeanor that the answer was yes.

But she decided to test him anyway.

"How many raised red stitches on a regulation baseball?"

"216."

Pure Cinema

Les images suffisent.

— René Clair

ITHIN THOSE DARK, FORBIDDING REFLECTIONS off the filthy waters of the bay, the listless seagulls scavenged aimlessly amid the waterfront debris—as that inexorable black dredge relentlessly gouged out the damp soft earth from the dark floor of the San Pedro mud flats—while, in the distance, the shoreline imperceptibly but inevitably collapsed itself back into the endless basin. And set against this stark and lifeless landscape, were all the useless, pathetic, disinterested people—silently, motionlessly, hypnotically resigned to their own consummate futility.

These were the Salvation Hunters.

And this particular night, half a century later, the audience comes in off the brisk autumn streets of the skyscraper city, into the Modern Art's cinema at Fifty-Third Street, only to find von Sternberg's slums, derelicts, and easy and excessive "fatalism" glossed over with the striking pictorial exuberance of Gheller's soft veils and photographic nets.

It was von Sternberg's first film, *The Salvation Hunters*, and, tonight, it was the first of the Modern's "von Sternberg Retrospective." Back in the fall of 1924, for five thousand dollars, he'd shot the film in three weeks, and, within a few months of its first screening, he'd acquired an international reputation. Yet despite its effectively brooding atmospheric composition and his rather enchanted rendering of the "sullen charm" of Georgia Hale, it was, as von Sternberg himself had admitted much later, "far less impressive today."

Nevertheless, it was still his "beginning" and his "promise," and the evening's cinema devotees chose to overlook its defects and to succumb to its pure visual artistry. Sitting there, in the artificial darkness, beneath the lightly flickering beam of the projection lamps, I found myself, during some of his interminably long static shots, glancing about me at von Sternberg's completely mesmerized audience.

Just two rows off to my right at the aisle, I noticed one particular man, elderly and rather dignified—dressed in a dark suit and wearing heavily tinted glasses—who actually seemed somehow transported or enraptured by the experience, and who would occasionally break off his "trance," run his hand meditatively through his thick white-and-gray hair, and then stare, it seemed to me, off from the screen. I suppose I was so struck by the man's behavior because his reaction was so dissimilar to my own. I'd seen the film several times before, and it only highlighted for me, as did von Sternberg's entire career, my own personal, but hardly unique, aesthetic crisis concerning the medium itself. I knew, only too well, how one can be mesmerized by alluring pictorial beauty, and I'd always considered von Sternberg's achievements most characteristic of this seduction—especially his later evocation of the haunting sensual face of Dietrich, that permanent erotic icon of this pathetic century, glimmering in his soft, shimmering, artificial lights and shadows.

Not far away in northern Jersey, I'd been raised and educated by a concerned and contented family that took the arts quite seriously, and later, when I went off to Rutgers, I fully expected to prepare for a lifetime directly related, in one way or another, to the literary arts. Yet, somehow, the cinema proved itself irresistible, and I was drawn away, and I eventually matriculated for graduate studies at UCLA in the Performing Arts. During the first year, von Sternberg joined the faculty for two semesters, and I enrolled in "The Film in Retrospect," helping G. Charles Essert compile his guide to the course which screened and reexamined von Sternberg's films. I found the man (von Sternberg) self-important, vindictive, arrogant, and only occasionally honest. But it was the overall shallowness of his intellect that disturbed me almost as much as his inadequate films and career. This was not because of the uniqueness of his failings, but because, as I've mentioned, he seemed a paradigm for all the films, for all the directors, and for the cinema itself. So within a few months of coming over fully to the cinematic "discipline," I found myself in a state of internal intellectual confusion, and, although I did maintain a certain faith in the occasional triumphs of Griffith, Bergman, and Resnais, I could never seem to forget Griffith's ringing indictment of the medium he'd dedicated his life to:

> When motion pictures have created something to
> compare with the plays of Euripides, or the works

of Homer or Shakespeare or Ibsen, or the music
of Handel or Bach, then let us call motion picture
entertainment an art—but not before then.

So it was in that frame of mind, after my second semester
at UCLA, that I wrote to Andrew Sarris at the Modern Art and
offered my services as a research intern for his upcoming von
Sternberg retrospective. When both Sarris and my graduate
committee approved the idea, I was, eventually, back East among
family and friends, enjoying the exhilarating rare breezes of the
city's coming autumn, and working with the Modern's perfectly
professional and congenial staff. Yet, despite all of these things,
my internal problems remained unresolved, and they, once again,
resurfaced as I sat in the darkness watching *The Salvation Hunters*
fade to its sudden and unlikely conclusion—faintly but improbably
hopeful in the midst of its picturesque despair and ennui.

During the intermission between screenings, I wandered
through the crowd and overheard the gush of praises and the
precious few reservations. Regardless, the crowd was pleasant
enough, and several of my friends had driven in from New
Jersey to make it especially so. Their "uninformed" but forthright
reactions and comments were the most interesting and accurate.
But, in time, our conversations inevitably turned to the "facts,"
what little was known, of the mysterious and disturbing break-in
that had occurred at my New York apartment two weeks earlier.
Then, as the lights suddenly dimmed, we retook our seats as
Professor Sarris made a few comments about von Sternberg's
second feature, the unreleased and "presumed lost," *A Woman
of the Sea,* the very film which had been the recent object of my
obsessive research. He pointed out that Chaplin's unabashed

admiration for *The Salvation Hunters* had induced him to hire
von Sternberg to direct Edna Purviance's "comeback" attempt.

Von Sternberg's second film, also called *The Seagull* (unrelated
to Chekhov), was shot on the Monterey seacoast in 1926 from
the director's original scenario: a simple love story set against the
dramatic background of the sea's violently changing modes and
patterns. The film displayed a breathtaking visual virtuosity, and
its extraordinary pictorial beauty clearly overwhelmed the "human
element" so highly valued by Charles Chaplin. Although several
scenes were reshot, Chaplin had finally decided to shelve the
project, but von Sternberg, in a defiant act of desperation, boldly
seized a print of the film and arranged for a private preview in
Beverly Hills. In his subsequent outrage, Chaplin either burned
the negative (according to John McCabe) or committed it to his
vaults (as von Sternberg always believed).

As Sarris continued his commentary about the missing
film, I, once again, noticed the same elderly man with the dark
glasses, who was now standing motionlessly but attentively at
the back of the theater. He listened very carefully as Professor
Sarris concluded his remarks about the missing film by citing two
especially pertinent quotes: the first was from John Grierson, who'd
attended that infamous screening in Beverly Hills and claimed that
A Woman of the Sea was "the most beautiful picture ever produced
in Hollywood." The second quote was from Robert Florey who
claimed that, although the film was "over the heads" of most of
its Beverly Hills audience, "it would have pleased the movie elite,
the *'Bœuf-sur-le-toit'* boys, Cocteau, Picabia, Buñuel, Dali, etc."

Naturally, the Modern's audience was greatly disappointed that
it couldn't see the vanished film, and certainly Grierson's appraisal
had stirred everyone's imagination about such an extraordinary

visual masterpiece that was now consigned to oblivion. Then, as the professor's commentary turned to address the director's next feature, *Underworld,* I noticed that the same elderly gentleman was now moving cautiously toward the door—gently and strangely running his left hand lightly across the surface of the back wall as he moved away. At the exit, he felt for the door and quickly left the theater as the next film began, and I wondered rather uneasily about this peculiar man who'd just passed, totally blind, through the image-rich palace of von Sternberg's cinema.

A few hours after the screening, when my friends finally drove off for the tunnel and home, I found myself walking the dark city streets alone, beneath the cold gray November night. My sublet was on East Sixty-Fourth, and, as I walked along, I again reconsidered all my frustrating failures to locate the missing film. When I'd first arrived in New York with the title of "researcher," I soon realized that Professor Sarris knew all that he needed to know about the extant films and that my status was really quite ambiguous. So I immediately offered to devote my time to searching for a print of *A Woman of the Sea* and attempting to clarify the intriguing mysteries surrounding its origin and fate. Sarris, always uncertain exactly what to do with me, generously agreed to support such an unlikely investigation.

I immediately wired Chaplin's representatives in London, politely requesting information about the film. Did it still exist? Could it be released for the retrospective? Etc. But my correspondence went unanswered, and all my subsequent transatlantic calls met with a cold and condescending disinterest. This, of course, again raised the often-asked question of why Chaplin had never once mentioned the project after 1926, not even in his autobiography. The three traditional suggestions

for his behavior still seemed feasible: 1) Artistic differences—
namely that Chaplin's sense of sentimental humanism could
never appreciate nor even comprehend von Sternberg's emphasis
on formal pictorial beauty, and that what Grierson had described
as "the visual patterns of the masts and rigging, the pattern of
sunlight on the drying nets, [and] the sculpturesque pattern of the
human figures" had only made a negative impression on Charles
Chaplin. 2) Purviance—the rumors that Chaplin's close friend had
been "outshone" by Eve Sothern were quite generous compared
to von Sternberg's veiled accusation that the fading actress had
been destroyed by alcohol, and that, as "her face disintegrated,
her eyes became helpless, and her body trembled like the leaf of
an aspen." 3) Vindictiveness—that Chaplin, infuriated by von
Sternberg's surreptitious screening, simply punished the arrogant
young director by shelving the project.

Von Sternberg was similarly rude. He'd left UCLA, and he
refused to respond to my correspondence, even my most innocuous
inquiries. Disheartened, but still not willing to abandon my efforts,
I started contacting everyone who'd, in any way, been connected
with the project. In this I was aided by my girlfriend, Lisa, who was
still living in LA, and we were quite thorough, but almost entirely
unproductive. Only Robert Florey offered tangible suggestions,
even hinting, quite mysteriously, that another print might yet
exist. He recommended that I try to contact von Sternberg's
editor, Joseph Marden, who'd left the industry in 1928 after a
debilitating accident and thereafter vanished. He also remarked,
rather offhandedly, that Marden had been to Paris in the 1920s
and, as a result, had entertained the most extreme "avant-garde"
notions regarding the cinema as art—as *le cinéma pur*—and
that he was also quite "unorthodox" politically.

Encouraged by the possibility, Lisa and I searched exhaustively for Marden on both coasts, but to no avail. Finally, in the remote possibility that his "unorthodox" politics might have earned him an agency file, I even went to the New York offices of the FBI at 26 Federal Plaza, but, again, turned up nothing. Finally, as the printing deadline for the retrospective's bulletin approached, I had to admit to myself that nothing of any real substance had been uncovered, and that Curtis Harrington's remarks in his exhaustive study of von Sternberg's films were still authoritative. Discouraged, I forced myself to write up my various notes, and totally disheartened, I went out for the evening. Later that same night, I returned to discover that my apartment had been broken into and that all my notes on *A Woman of the Sea* had been stolen. It's quite difficult to explain the effects of such a violation of one's privacy, and all the vague implications that it suggested about my research. Something was clearly at stake in all this, and, suddenly I felt threatened and vulnerable.

The next day, I wrote my notes for Sarris from memory, drove to my parent's home, and, without their knowledge, procured my father's service revolver from his desk drawer. I suppose that I was overreacting, but it was impossible to ignore my intimations of some kind of potential danger. Then, exactly two days later, unexpectedly, my notes arrived in the morning mail in a large manila envelope, intact and without either comment or alteration. Despite this comforting turn of events, I still maintained my guard, and, as the screenings approached, I continued, without success, to follow up my last few remaining leads.

But now the retrospective had begun, and *A Woman of the Sea* had passed. As the night grew colder, I gladly came in from the deserted city streets and entered my apartment building. Very slowly, I walked down its dark cool corridors, moving within the harsh night-shadows and soft security lamplights. Finally, after making the last turn, as I reached out for my apartment door, I immediately sensed that it was happening again. The door was unlocked. As my body reflexively flushed with the burning cold-flashings of adrenaline, I knelt down quietly in the hallway, listened to the silence beyond the door, and carefully removed the Colt .38 from my briefcase. The weapon felt rather cold in my hand, but I was resolved.

I stood up slowly and cautiously entered the apartment. Within, it was mostly dark, and perfectly quiet, although a few gray night-lights softly filtered inside from the outside windows. Without a sound, I came up behind the man where he sat immobile in a chair in the center of the room. Then I raised the gun to within a few inches of his right temple, cocked it, and asked in a calm but resolute voice:

"What do you want?"

The figure, as if emerging from some uncertain reverie, slowly, without any visible indication of fear, turned to face me. It was the elderly blind man from the von Sternberg screening, seemingly harmless and even vulnerable in the dark.

He spoke:

"I'm sorry."

He seemed sincerely concerned, as if realizing for the first time that his actions might have caused me serious alarm. Then he explained:

"My name is Joseph Marden." There was a pause. "Will you hear me out?"

Suddenly, I grew rather embarrassed of my threatening position. I lowered the gun, backed off to the couch, and sat down and waited.

"I suppose," he hesitated, as if considering exactly where he should begin, "I suppose I should recall my youth—to put everything in its proper perspective."

Then, quite calmly and thoughtfully, he reflected back over his life, speaking softly in a most precise narrative that made a deep and permanent impression. "I was born into a family of accomplished, let's say, first-rate musicians, and, although I eventually ended up at Julliard, I was never fully comfortable with the aesthetic 'obligations' of my upbringing. Later, when it became clear that Wilson intended to enter the war, I quit school and enlisted in the Expeditionary Force. My division saw action at St. Mihiel, and we followed Black Jack into the Argonne Forest. We were very fortunate, suffering relatively few casualties before the Germans capitulated. Then, after the Armistice, I went to Paris.

"Those years of Post-War Paris were, as you know, incredibly dynamic times. War was over—some claimed forever—and the arts quickly reassumed their ascendant position in Parisian life. The great French capital was flooded with young artists and outrageous ideas: Cubism, Dadaism, and Surrealism; Orphism, Expressionism, and Futurism; Abstract art, Freud, and Marx. But of all the now-flourishing arts, it was the cinema that was the most seized upon as the artistic medium with the greatest potential, promise, and possibility. It was an amazing period of frenetic experimentation and the boldest theorizing, a time of excess and self-indulgence—all led by the legendary avant-garde: Delluc, Desnos, Gance, and Clair; Epstein, Man Ray, Duchamp, and Léger; Dulac, Renoir, Buñuel, and countless others. In the midst of all this wild activity, there were really only a few talented individuals, who were surrounded by a flood of enthusiasts and pretenders inspired by Griffith, the Germans, Sjöström, and the seemingly limitless possibilities their work suggested."

Gently, I lay the gun down on the couch as the man continued. Although he tried to speak with a certain objectivity, there was also an undeniable excitement of memory, combined with some vague, almost tragic sense of remorse.

"Of course, I was no exception to the seductions of the cinema, and I spent my afternoons at the Studio des Ursulines and my evenings in the noisy cafés engaged in aesthetic 'upmanship' with the likes of Clair, Brunius, Picabia, Mitry, and even, on his occasional visits, the brooding young von Sternberg. During those years, I managed to support myself with the piano, and I started cutting films for both the declining Gaumont Studios and for the many independent abstract shorts that were being produced by my friends, especially René Clair. I even had, for example, an editorial influence on *Entr'acte*, the 1924 sensation and scandal which was once characterized as the quintessential exemplar of *'le cinéma pur.'*

"Yes, 'Purity!' That was the watchword of the Parisian twenties, and it was paid due homage by every artist and theorist in the city. Kant had once had his 'pure reason,' and James and Avenarius had discussed their versions of 'pure experience,' but it was Valéry who, in 1920, stirred artistic imaginations with his almost casual mention of *'la poésie pure'* in the forward to a colleague's book. Immediately, the concept took on a life of its own, reaching an amazing crescendo, several years later, not long before I left Paris, when the Jesuit Henri Brémond gave his incendiary lecture at the Institut de France. For Brémond almost everything was 'impure':

narrative, subject, reason, sensibility, description, and, of course, language itself. His inevitable conclusion, *'la poésie pure est silence,'* reduced the poet to utter silence, forlornly clutching his pure, blank, and unblemished white pages. Although less dogmatic, and much more sophisticated, Valéry similarly believed that the 'pure' poem was an illogical impossibility, but he finally concluded that the very 'composing process' itself—and the activity's actual effect on the composing poet—was all that really mattered. However, if 'the *act of creation* is the principal thing,' as Valéry had contended, then everyone except for the artist was excluded from the realms of art. As Eliot would later recall, M. Louis Bolle accused such aesthetic solipsism as 'intellectual narcissism.'

"But as for the cinephiles, *'le cinéma pur,'* as discussed by Clair in his articles in *Le Théâtre et Comœdia illustré,* was less ambitious. It was essentially the total glorification of the 'image' as an end in itself—at the expense of narrative, character, sound, etc. Only the visual image and the 'rhythm' of those images was the pure, inherent, and permanent substance of the medium. Surely, Clair's *Entr'acte,* whatever its numerous faults, is best seen in the light of Clair's famous definition that translates: 'a fragment of film becomes "pure cinema" as soon as a sensation is aroused through purely visual means.' Although most of the cinematic products of that period, as with all avant-garde movements, were pretentious failures that were soon well-forgotten, there were occasionally isolated successes, like Kirsanov's *Ménilmontant* with its stunning visuals and the mysteriously moving performance by Nadia Sibirskaïa."

Then Marden's voice trailed off as he caught himself digressing in his memories, and he was quite direct about it.

"Is this tiresome?"

"Not at all." Since I'd clearly reassured him, I encouraged him further, "Please, take your time."

So he did.

"So I was not indifferent to the intellectual currents of those times, and before I left Paris, late one night at the Café Sarrasine, Clair, Brunius, and I speculated about what might be the absolute 'apogee' of cinematic experience. I proposed that Valéry's 'narcissism' of the poet, the creating writer himself, should be removed from the author and transferred, in the cinema, to the narcissism of the 'exceptional' viewer. I suggested that the 'absolute optimum aesthetic experience' would be for the most sophisticated viewer to screen the 'purest' film in Clair's sense of visual beauty, and to screen the film entirely *alone,* in silence, and only *once*—as a kind of 'pure perception'—and then to destroy the once-seen film."

Marden stopped and looked over in my direction.

"However these notions might strike one today, I can assure you that Clair was extremely intrigued, and we immediately planned to produce two strikingly visual shorts—one for each of us. Then we planned to view our individual films separately, and then burn the negatives and prints together."

Marden looked away and paused, as if disgusted with himself. Then he started again, softly, emphatically.

"It was, of course, all *rubbish.* Just self-indulgent, egocentric nonsense, entirely typical of the pseudo-intellectual faddism of the time. The city was flush with young intellectual frauds and pretenders, each trying to outdo the others, each trying in the most childish ways to assert some kind of self-satisfied but unfounded ascendancy over the 'bourgeois'—while, all the while, endlessly mouthing only the slightest variations of the same shallow contemporary clichés, and always doing so without even the most elementary artistic or historical grounding. Faddism in France is a kind of ephemeral 'art' form, and aesthetic theory is its haven for the poser, the dilettante, and the camp-follower. Never forget, young man: the truest test of the artificiality of any intellectual enterprise is its terminology, and the city in those days reeked with such nondescript and obfuscating pretensions as: 'epiphenomenal,' 'paroxistic,' 'oneiric,' 'animistic,' 'theogenistic,' and all the rest of it."

Marden trailed off. Then, he looked again in my direction.

"Do I have to tell you what happened?"

Since there was only silence, he eventually looked away, off into the far dark corner of the room, and explained.

"Von Sternberg offered me a job, so I went to Los Angeles where I was immediately put to work cutting the rushes for *The Seagull*. From the very first of those daily screenings of von Sternberg's relentless retakes, it was clear to me and everyone else that Chaplin would never allow such unabashed 'formalism' to attach itself to his international reputation. The visuals were spectacularly breathtaking, and Purviance, despite all her problems, looked perfectly beautiful. But none of this would matter to Chaplin, and the inevitable clash of these two tyrannical, self-centered, and vengeful personalities doomed the project even as the shooting continued and several scenes were reshot. Cutting the film became a mere formality, and my personal dislike for both men, especially in contrast with the easy, if artificial, camaraderie of Paris, did little to make my efforts tolerable."

Then Marden paused, momentarily, and reflected.

"So I did it. I did what I should never have done and that which I have ever since regretted, but also that which actually made no impact whatsoever on anything beyond my own suffering sense of integrity. I simultaneously cut *two* versions of the film: one for my own purposes and one for Chaplin's scrap pile. His final decision not to release the film surprised no one, but von Sternberg's defiant 'secret' preview in Beverly Hills caught everyone off-guard. Von Sternberg, naturally, never consulted with me, so he took the wrong cut and screened the inferior, although still quite beautiful, version of the film."

"Are you saying that *none* of them, including Grierson, ever saw the final cut?"

"That's correct."

I didn't know what to say, or how to react, so I said nothing.

"Then Chaplin seized the once-screened version, and he either burned it or sank it into his vaults."

I waited for more.

"Then late one night at United Artists, I sat alone in the darkness and the absolute silence, and I watched the most beautiful film ever made—certainly weak in narrative and motivation, but unsurpassed in pictorial beauty. But afterwards, theory or no theory, I discovered that I couldn't burn it, and although I didn't realize it at the time, I was inhibited from doing so by a deep-rooted sense of shame. Finally, I locked up the reels and pushed it out of my mind.

"During the subsequent year, a great deal happened, and many serious doubts about myself, my beliefs, and the cinema itself became paramount in my life. I was, it's certainly true, greatly affected by the death of my father that following winter. I was also shaken by the irrefutable documentation of all the tragic events currently taking place in the Soviet Union, and I was aesthetically depressed by the increasing failures and increasing commercialization of Parisian film society.

"Then, in November 1928, at MGM, while screening Dreyer's *Joan* for the very first and last time, a powerful flash fire in the studio projection booth leapt into my eyes and burned them closed forever. Whatever the physical cause of my blindness, it was ironic retribution. My eyes closed forever with the silent era, and I was never able to experience a 'talking sound' film. Very soon afterwards, I left the industry for good, although I've always kept up with the medium as a part of a wider determination to reeducate myself in the broader sense—and to, thus, compensate for the follies of my youth."

"And then?" I asked.

"I returned to music. I've played the keyboards throughout the city for many years, and must," he felt for his watch, "play at a service at St. Stephen's early in the morning."

He rose to leave.

"Young man, I'm not embittered. I've come to fully accept my position in life and to atone for my previous failings. This public confession was my last responsibility."

"Do others know?"

"They could only suspect."

"Do you want it known?"

He hesitated.

"I'm not really sure. You'll have to decide, young man. But if you do so, be certain that what was once done in vanity and foolishness is never portrayed, in any way, as attractive."

I understood perfectly. I walked over in the darkness, took his arm, and led him to the door. Then I finally asked him what seemed to me the most important question of all.

"What does the cinema really have to offer?"

Marden reflected a moment.

"I remember that Clair once wrote that the *real* secret of the cinema, its true inherent charm, lay in its ability to 'speak of love.'"

He left off right there, and I was certain that he'd very consciously chosen not to answer my question more directly. Then, just before he took his leave, he shook my hand and looked directly into my eyes.

"I'm sorry that I arranged for your notes to be taken. It was wrong, but I felt that if this story should ever come to light, it should be after the principals were dead."

Then he turned around and walked away down the shadowed corridor, gently feeling the wall as he moved along. I stood and watched him go, feeling that to offer assistance would have been an impertinence.

★ ★ ★

IN HIS LAST CORRESPONDENCE, many years later, Marden again issued a strong warning about the excesses of theory: "Beware of Saussurism! I sometimes think that this entire century is nothing more than the sorry history of that particular *ism*'s insidious infiltration and eventual tyranny over every other discipline— quickly strangling the life, the common sense, and the humanity from the endeavors of man." During his last illness, he seemed to have forgotten that, by now, my own interest in the cinema was, as his own had become, concerned, yet definitely at a remove.

When word of his death finally arrived, Lisa and I flew to New York and attended a quite magnificent requiem Mass at St. Stephen's. As I listened to the very same organ that he'd once played with unparalleled humility, virtuosity, and rapture, I reflected on how his many kindnesses and talents had, over the years, made him so many close and caring friends. Yet Marden died without family, and I found myself, with some surprise, the executor of his will. A portion of his remaining assets was dispersed among his closest friends, and all the rest went to the Society for the Preservation of Film Classics. Similarly, his rare collections and film journals from the early twenties were also donated to the society's library.

So I spent several days cataloging and packaging the books in his large apartment. Then, late one summer afternoon, as the sunlight slowly sank beneath the skyline, I discovered the rusted canisters amid the many piles of dust-covered books and journals and files. As the motes rose gently, shimmering in the soft summer light, I sat back into a comfortable chair and held in my hands the forgotten reels of that long lost film simply marked: *A Woman of the Sea.* I suppose that I might have reflected on the transitory nature of man's achievement or on the impermanence of the medium itself, but I remember feeling nothing more than a certain kind of awkward sadness. I opened up the canisters, and discovered, as expected, the disintegrated, totally decayed, remains of the once-seen masterpiece. The cellulose nitrate had totally decomposed itself into an unrecognizable and indescribable dark mass of grotesquely congealed material and some powdery dust.

I rose up immediately and took the reels down to the furnace in the building's basement. Alone in the dark hot underground, I opened its heavy iron doors and tossed in the unsalvageable remnants of another era. Highly flammable, its nitrate gave out a sudden and violent flash and blast of heat—forceful, gently beautiful, pure, and then gone forever.

CALIFORNIA

Outline

HE WAS SITTING ON THE BEACH READING Travis McGee, wasting his life away. Sure, every once in a while, Eric would have some passing guilts, but not too many. Most of the time, he didn't think about it at all, trusting in the unthought-about conviction that somewhere in the deep and more responsible back end of his consciousness, he was fully expecting, someday, that he'd break out of his current three-years-and-still-running funk, and do a bit more with his life than hang out at the beach, pretend to write his guidebook, and watch the pretty girls playing volleyball on beautiful Manhattan Beach, sometimes known as the "Wimbledon of Volleyball," just south of Santa Monica and north of Redondo.

There was a time when he'd wanted to be a *real* writer, someone like John D. MacDonald, or, better yet, someone like Ross Macdonald, but he just couldn't handle the plots. He could *write* well enough—who couldn't?—but he couldn't work out a plotted story no matter how hard he tried, and no matter how many outlines he worked on, so he finally gave up. His once-upon-a-time fiancée had once said with absolute authority, "If there's no plot, there's no point," and Eric agreed. Irene, among many other things, was a librarian, and she'd read a billion books, and she often tried to help him out. She gave him story ideas and "ending" ideas, and she even wrote him an outline once, right in the middle of their ugly little breakup, but he'd never even bothered to read it. Eric knew his limitations, and, for the time being, he was fine with being a worthless beach bum.

"You got the time?"

She'd come up the beach from the volleyball courts with the morning sun glaring behind her. Given her tan and her lean muscularity, maybe 13 percent body fat, it seemed obvious that she was competing in the tournament. She was very pretty, wearing a red spandex bikini, actually a Nautica designer two-piece.

Eric glanced down at his blanket, pushed up his polarized shades, and pulled the watch out of his Dodgers' cap.

"It's 10:15."

She thought about it a moment, then she looked down at his paperback.

"*The Deep Blue Good-By,*" she said pensively, and smiled, "I bet you think you're a lot like Travis?"

She was kidding, of course, both friendly and flirty, and referring to the detective-hero, the "salvage consultant," of John D. MacDonald's Travis McGee novels.

"Not as tough," Eric admitted, "but luckier. Who wants to live in Florida?"

She liked that, and she kept things going.

"I thought the book was a little too predictable," she decided, "and I also feel that Travis is a bit too self-congratulatory."

"That seems an odd word to hear from a nearly naked woman on a California beach," Eric kidded.

But she didn't mind.

She smiled again and shrugged.

"I bet I know more odd words than you do."

Eric didn't doubt it, and he didn't contest it.

Then she looked off behind her into the sun, and Eric followed her gaze and saw the other beach girl—this one in a striking yellow bikini, probably a Nike, with a pair of small binoculars strapped around her neck. She had short-cropped blond hair, and the friends waved to each other.

"Enjoy the book," the closer one said, "I gotta go."

"What's your name?"

"Dallas."

"Texas is my second favorite state," he tried.

She smiled again.

"Why not come and watch us play tomorrow?" she suggested. "We could use a fan."

Without waiting for a response, she walked away, into the California sun. When she met up with her friend, they looked, in the distance, almost identical, except for the hair. Both were perfect, young, beautiful, and athletic, and they reminded him of Irene, except that they both had "beach" tans, and she'd always had a "tennis" tan.

> *Outline (rough):*
> *1. Some directionless guy meets a mysteriously attractive young woman, and they plan to meet again.*

The next day was the first day of the prelims for the AVP Manhattan Beach Open, the premier event in the volleyball season, but Dallas and her partner never showed up for their match, and they were disqualified. Sam Harper, whom Eric had known since they were kids at Pacific Grammar, was running the tournament again this year, and he told Eric everything he knew, which wasn't much: her name was Dallas Carr, and she and her partner were "walk-ons" from Santa Barbara.

Sam shrugged, Eric shrugged too, and that was the end of it.

With nothing to do, Eric hung around the courts for a while, watching a few matches, before he headed back home to his fourteen-bedroom "mansion" in the upscale Hill Section of Manhattan Beach where he ate the delicious lunch that Dorotea, his Salvadorian cook and sometimes housecleaner, had left in the refrigerator for him. When Eric was full and satisfied, he got more curious, and, since he had nothing else planned, he googled "Dallas Carr" and learned that she'd been killed yesterday in a parking lot outside La Cumbre Plaza, a rather ritzy shopping mall in Santa Barbara. There weren't many details in the brief online report posted on the website for *The Santa Barbara News-Press.* It seemed as though Dallas had been putting something in the back of her SUV when another shopper accidentally backed up and crushed her between the cars. Hopefully, she'd died instantly, but Eric really didn't know.

A bit numb, he stared out the oceanside back window of his dad's old study and looked at the waves. It was something he could do for hours on end, especially since the death of his mother a few years ago.

Back in the late 1940s, right after the war, Eric's grandfather had made a fortune in real estate. Years later, Eric's dad had more than tripled the wealth he'd inherited, without ever, apparently, sacrificing either his good nature or his unfailing integrity. He was a good father, maybe even a great father, and his only fault was that he died unexpectedly of an aneurism when Eric was only thirteen. But it was really his mother's death, just three years ago, that had really rocked Eric's world. He was rich, definitely good-looking, far from stupid, likeable, and only twenty-eight years old, but all the "life" and all of his ambition had drained right out of him. He broke off his engagement, minimized his social life, stopped dating entirely, gave up on church, and seemed perfectly content to feel sorry for himself.

So he stared at the ocean a lot.

> *2. When the girl doesn't show up, the guy attempts to track her down and learns that she's dead.*

Later that afternoon, Eric got curious again, and he did some more Internet snooping, learning that Dallas had a sister living at the beach near Hermosa. So he pulled out his candy-apple-red Corvette and headed south. He liked Hermosa, which was just a couple of miles from Manhattan Beach, and he'd even lived in one of its tiny beach houses for a few months after he'd dropped out of college. Eric had grown up a completely obsessed surfer kid, but when he crushed his ankle on a jetty up north in Half Moon Bay, the party was over. Even now, he still had a bit of a limp and occasional pains, but he didn't mind it that much, either now or back then.

When he was seventeen, the accident made him face up to the fact that he needed to go to college, and he'd always wanted to write short stories, ever since Ray Bradbury had signed his copy of *Death is a Lonely Business* at Vroman's Bookstore in Pasadena when he was twelve years old. Both before and after that meeting, Eric had always been able to concoct the most fantastically clever stories, entertaining his mother, his sister, and all his friends at the beach, who seemed to take it for granted that he had the "gift."

So he flew off to the University of Hawaii, a stone's throw from Waikiki, and majored in creative writing.

Where else would a much-too-wealthy ex-surfer guy go?

Out on the islands, he greatly enjoyed reading the great books—Chaucer and the Brontës and Melville and Faulkner—but his writing classes were a real letdown. Eventually, he came to realize that these modern creative writing programs *really could* teach people how to write decent sentences. If you do enough of it—if you write a few million pages—you'll eventually develop a nice personal literary style. In truth, any moron can learn to write, which Eric certainly did. But, on the other hand, only one-in-a-skillion can actually tell a decent story, and since you can't really teach "plot"—just like you can't teach somebody to be a great storyteller—all of his teachers talked endlessly about "character" and "setting" and "meaning" and "description" and all the rest of the stuff that's perfectly useless without some kind of a plot to hang on to. So the teachers encouraged them all to write "resolutionless" stories, since that's all they could write themselves, and they even convinced the students, and, apparently, themselves as well, that it was much more like "real life" that way, and that, paradoxically, it was also "harder" to do.

All of which Eric knew was perfect crap.

So after two years, he dropped out, flew home, lived at Hermosa for a few months, and then tried it again at Santa Cruz. But it was just more of the same. Although, the second time around, he decided to brass it out for his mother's sake, but he definitely gave up on "literary" fiction. Yes, he still loved Hawthorne and Borges and Greene and the rest of them, but, in today's world, it seemed that only the mystery people took plot very seriously. So he tried to construct story lines like Ross

Macdonald, always remembering what Aristotle had said, which Eric felt was the most important thing that *anybody* had ever said about writing, that "the ending should be unexpected but not unbelievable," and he tried, and he failed, and he finally gave up. So nowadays he told anybody who bothered to ask "So what are you doing with yourself?" that he was writing a nonfiction guidebook about the Southern California beaches, something he knew quite a bit about.

Eric pulled his Vette convertible in front of Violet Carr's beach house, and he got out of the car. He knew he shouldn't be here, but he was, and he wasn't about to wimp out now. When he knocked on the door, a young woman, whom he concluded was an older and nowhere-near-as-fit and obviously emotionally distraught version of Dallas, opened the door and waited patiently.

"I'm a friend of Dallas," he said, "and I thought I'd stop by and see if I can help in any way."

It was perfectly obvious that the last thing the grieving sister needed was some "friend" she'd never seen before, but she was too nice to send him away, and she invited him in. But once she'd made her mistake, she, quite apologetically, spent most of her time sobbing softly in her bedroom and packing for the drive north to Santa Barbara. Which left Eric abandoned on the beat-up living room couch with Violet's surfer-dude-boyfriend Mickey. To pass the time, Eric conjured up a couple of stories about some stuff he'd supposedly done with Dallas, but it was clear that Mickey couldn't have cared less, so they ended up talking about the waves at Malibu, Rincon, and Steamer Lane. Mickey was remarkably stoic about everything that was going on around him, which seemed rather suspicious to Eric, which was perfectly ridiculous since he knew absolutely nothing about these people.

In the midst of one of their conversational lulls, Eric looked over at a framed picture of Mickey and Violet and another girl wearing mouse ears at Disneyland, and he picked up the picture.

"Who's this?" he asked stupidly, but not without purpose.

Eric pointed to the second girl, and Mickey looked at him like he was an idiot.

"That's Dallas," he said.

Eric nodded, as calm as calm could be. Then he stood up and walked to the door.

"Tell Violet that she's in my thoughts, and I'll see her at the wake," he said with sincerity, immediately leaving the beach house, not even bothering to look back and see if Mickey's face was clouded with a mess of suspicions.

> *3. He goes to talk to the dead girl's sister, and he sees a photograph of the "real" Dallas.*

The next morning, Eric weaved his way past the countless desks at the Parker Center in downtown LA, heading for his sister's cubicle. Already an assistant detective, Jane Kincaid was moving up fast, and Eric was proud of her success at LAPD despite their estrangement. For some reason, Jane had really liked Irene, whom she hardly knew at all, and when Eric broke things off, Jane felt that he'd handled it badly, even "cruelly," which was certainly true. Eventually, after their mother died, Jane got very impatient with Eric's moping around—his refusal to "get over it." She'd look at him back then and say, "I loved Mom just as much as you!" After all, she was the oldest, and their mother was a saint, but there comes a time when you have to "get on" with things, which was exactly what she was doing at LAPD, and exactly what Eric *wasn't* doing, choosing, instead, to waste his life away like a spoiled brat.

"Mother would *hate* that," she'd said the last time they talked, about a year ago, and she was exactly right.

Jane was always coming up with "theories" about everything, which always began, "You know what I think?" and one day, back before she'd given up on him, she said, "You know what I think?" and he waited, and she told him.

"I think you can't write because of those damned schools. I think those creative writing classes destroyed your creativity—and your imagination. You could always tell clever stories before you ran off to Hawaii."

When Eric didn't respond, Jane added yet another theory, as a kind of addendum.

"I also think Mom's sickness contributed as well. Why shouldn't you get a bit blocked for a while?"

"I don't believe in writers' block," Eric said stupidly.

When he finally arrived at Jane's desk, she looked up from a pile of papers. She didn't seem overly surprised, and she wasn't especially hostile, and she listened to his "Dallas" story.

"I'm being set up," Eric explained.

"For what?" she wondered, but he had no idea, so he just shrugged.

"I talked to Sam down at the open," he continued, "and he said that her teammate's name was 'Aggie Sayers.' What does that tell you?"

Jane couldn't help but laugh.

"Yeah, Agatha Christie and Dorothy Sayers," Eric pointed out the obvious.

"Obviously," Jane said. "So what? Someone's just goofing on

you. They took the name of the real Dallas, who died in Santa Barbara two days ago, and they used it to mess with you a bit. So what? There's no crime here, Eric, just a sick joke."

Eric sat there and let her have her say.

"So what do you want from me, anyway?" she asked, "We're a bit busy around this nuthouse today."

"I think it's Irene," Eric explained. "I think she's behind it, and I'd like you to find out where she is."

Which was still a sore subject.

"She's in Tucson," Jane reminded him with some irritation. "She went out there to room with an old UCLA girlfriend after you dumped her. And I'm sure you know, just as well as I do, that she got another library job in Tucson."

"She did," Eric agreed, "but she's not there anymore. I called the library this morning. And she's not in the Tucson phone book."

Jane seemed bored.

"I think we should leave the poor girl alone."

Then a departmental clerk came over to the desk with some papers for Jane to sign, and Eric waited patiently. When the guy finally left, Jane was getting ready to dismiss her brother, but he didn't let her.

"You need to know something about Mom," he said, and that definitely got her attention.

"Unlike you, and unlike me for much too long, Mom saw right through Irene. She saw the darkness, and she sensed the violence."

"Violence?" Jane cut him off, more surprised than anything else.

"That's right," Eric assured her, "I saw it a number of times."

Jane was ready to listen.

"Two nights before Mom died from that lousy cancer in that lousy bed, she took my hand, and she told me that she had one dying wish. She wanted me to end things with Irene. She saw nothing but trouble down that road, and I knew in my heart she was right, and I said yes, and three days later, right after the funeral, I broke things off with Irene."

Jane was quiet and thoughtful for a moment.

"Why didn't you tell me this before?"

Eric shrugged.

"You'd already made up your mind that I was the villain in the story, and, besides, I was so messed up with losing Mom that I just didn't care."

There was another brief silence between the older sister and the younger brother. Finally, Jane spoke again, just like a cop.

"I'll find her."

4. Convinced that he's being set up, possibly by his ex-fiancée, he tries to track her down.

Leaving LAPD central, Eric drove east to San Bernardino to talk to "Harry" Doyle, actually "Harriet" Doyle, who was the only friend that Irene had ever talked about from her youth in San Bernardino. As he was cruising along Route 10, Eric remembered the first time, five years ago, when he met Irene, with a group of mutual friends, at the annual USC-UCLA football game at the Rose Bowl. At the time, he'd recently come home from Santa Cruz to "write," and Irene was studying library science at UCLA. Although both Eric's dad and his sister had gone to USC, he'd opted to get out of town for his stint in Hawaii, but he was still loyal to the Trojans, and they won big that day.

But Irene didn't care about football. She was tall, and slender, and graceful, with a tennis girl's body. She was also smart and beautiful, and, although she was a bit more "serious" than Eric, they hit it off right away, especially discussing books and writers and writing. Like Eric, she also liked the big boys—Dostoevsky and Shakespeare and O'Neill—but she loved the mysteries best of all, and she knew a lot about writing. She also knew a lot about tragedy, having lost her twin sister in a drowning accident when they were twelve, and then losing her mother two years later when the woman, apparently inconsolable over the loss of her child, ran off to Mexico and abandoned her husband and Irene. Eventually, her dad, a nice-guy geological researcher, died from a totally unexpected heart failure, and Irene was suddenly all alone in the world at seventeen and heading off for UCLA.

As Eric cruised down the highway, he remembered lots of other stuff. He remembered watching her play tennis, their trips to Catalina, her love of raspberry ice cream, and their all-night discussions about *The Chill* and a million other books. He also remembered the lovely scent of her dark hair, and her gentle touch and gentle lips, and the liquid passion in her violet eyes. He also remembered the time that she attacked him, totally unexpectedly, after a reception in Santa Monica. She came after him in a violent rage, shaking with venom, with her fists flailing. Eric somehow managed to catch her wrists in his hands, but she kicked him in the shins, and she even tried to bite him. When she finally burned out, she dropped to the floor and cried like a little girl, explaining not-too-coherently that she was jealous about some girl who'd talked to him a bit too "intently" at the reception. So he held her close, and comforted her, and forgave her.

But he didn't forget.

He was always aware that "it" was still there, somewhere within her—a rage beneath the surface—and his mother had glimpsed it, or somehow sensed it, and when she told him to put an end to things, he did.

Harriet Doyle had been remarkably easy to track down this morning. Her father owned a string of florist shops in San Bernardino, and, although she was married now, she was still working for her father. When Eric rang her up after breakfast, he told her that Irene seemed to be missing, and that some of her friends were worried about her and doing their best to find her. Since he was passing, by coincidence, through San Bernardino this afternoon, he'd love to stop and talk. Harriet was friendly, concerned, and ready to help. She agreed to meet Eric at Alfredo's on Baseline Street, and he pulled into the lot at 2:15.

"I'll wear a pink carnation," she'd said this morning, and he spotted her immediately. She was very pretty, and, surprisingly, she wore the flower in her hair.

Back when Eric and Irene were dating, Irene talked incessantly about her "best friend," but Eric never actually met "Harry," which, at first, seemed very peculiar. But the truth was, as Eric soon learned, although Irene floated in and out of several UCLA social circles, she really didn't have any friends.

Eric sat down, smiling across the red and white checkered tablecloth, and he did his best to put Harriet at ease, saying things like: "Well, she's done this kind of thing before," and "We're not really *that* worried," and "I'm sure she'll pop up soon."

"Besides," Eric explained, "I've heard so much about you over the years that it's great to finally meet you."

Harriet was fine with that.

She was, as it turned out, just as thoughtful and engaging as she was pretty, and Eric gently encouraged her to talk about Irene and their childhood friendship, which she did very comfortably. She told Eric about a number of "silly" teenage pranks and stories and happenings, and it was perfectly obvious that Harriet still cared for her childhood friend, whom she described as charming, clever, a bit too serious, and sometimes rather brazen. She also remembered Irene's twin, Adella, whom they all called Della, who'd drowned in the boating accident. The twins were identicals, and so much alike that even Harry, who was with them all the time, had trouble telling them apart.

"How did she deal with her sister's death?"

"Not too well," Harry remembered, "she seemed numb for several months, but she eventually came out of it. Of course, it caused her problems."

Eric wasn't sure if he should press her about the "problems," so he didn't, and he changed the subject.

"If you were her best friend," he wondered out loud, "why haven't we ever met?"

This clearly made Harriet a bit uneasy, but she decided to tell the truth.

"We had a falling out in high school," she explained, "in junior year."

"Can I ask what happened?"

Harriet took a moment to decide, and then she answered the question with another question.

"I guess you know about her violent streak?" she asked, clearly assuming that Eric *did* know.

"Yes."

"Well, I saw her go kind of berserk one night on another girl after we went to the movies together. It scared me quite a bit, and I told my mom about it, and it scared her even more, and she told me I had to cut Irene off."

"And you did?"

"I did."

Harriet was clearly rethinking her past.

"But I still feel somewhat uneasy about it," she admitted. "We all make mistakes, and considering what she'd been through in her life, it's small wonder that she's got some issues. Some buried rage."

Eric agreed.

5. In the meantime, he begins to look into his ex-fiancée's past.

After getting back home from San Bernardino, Eric walked into his huge empty house, and there was a phone message waiting:

"This is Detective Allan Hunter leaving a message for Mr. Eric Kincaid. You've probably heard about the death of Violet Carr last night, and since you spoke to her sometime last night, I'd like to ask you a few questions. I'll call again later—or stop by. Thanks."

But Eric didn't believe it. He was now convinced that he knew *exactly* what was going on—and how he should deal with it.

He immediately went upstairs into his walk-in attic, found his "Irene" box, sorted through the letters, concert programs, photographs, CDs, wedding announcements, and all the other "stuff" from their three years together. Then he found what he was looking for: the unopened envelope marked on the outside, "Here's an outline for the writer who can't write."

The truth of Irene's sarcasm still hurt, and Eric remembered the day she'd come by the house, screaming and banging on the front door before she finally slipped the envelope through the front-door slot. Even though she never caught a glimpse of Eric that night, she *knew* that he was somewhere inside the house, but Eric was afraid of her. He just wanted her to leave him alone and go away, and, finally, she did. From an upstairs window, he surreptitiously watched her as she walked down the driveway, looking beautiful as always. Then she got in her car, drove away, and he never saw her again. Until yesterday on the beach, and now she was coming again, and he knew exactly what she wanted.

Eric shut the box, went downstairs, and took his father's Ruger KP93 from the desk and pulled out his box of nine millimeters. When he was done loading the bullets, Eric went back online and found a much more thorough account of the accidental death of Dallas Carr, including, as he now fully expected, the fact that she'd died early in the morning.

Hours before he'd meet the imposter Dallas on Manhattan Beach.

Then Eric called his sister at her condo in El Segundo, and he moved into the living room to wait for Irene. Unlocking the front door, he sat down on the couch facing the entrance, and he placed the Ruger on the end table right beside him.

> *6. Convinced that he knows why his ex-fiancée is coming after him, he gets the "outline" and prepares.*

But there was still something else that Eric needed to decide, and he looked down at the unopened envelope in his hands.

"Oh, the hell with it," he said to himself, and he placed the unopened envelope on the table next to the Ruger.

Why bother to read the outline?

Who wants to know the ending before it comes?

So Eric decided, for better or worse, to play it as it lay.

Sixteen minutes later, a striking young woman pushed open the front door of the mansion and came into the living room. She was blond, perfectly lovely, and she wore an expensive evening dress, probably a Vera Wang, and she carried a Colt XSE in her right hand, which she immediately pointed at Eric's face.

"Do you know who I am?" she asked calmly.

"Yes, 'Aggie Sayers.' Is it a wig?"

Irene, still keeping her Colt pointed directly at Eric, reached up with her left hand and pulled off the short blond wig and let it drop to the floor. Her own dark cropped hair was a bit disheveled, but she still looked beautiful, although, obviously looking the part, she also looked quite deranged.

Then Irene gestured with her Colt to the envelope resting on the table next to Eric.

"Did you read it?"

"No."

"Do you know how it ends?"

"No, but I know what you did."

Oddly enough, she seemed pleased.

"Good for you,' she said, not without sarcasm.

"So who played Dallas on the beach?" Eric wondered.

"Some beach-bunny 'actress-model,'" Irene explained dismissively. "But aren't they all? They'll do anything for a few hundred bucks, but I must admit, I thought she did quite well."

"She did," Eric agreed.

"But I was quite disappointed to see that you were reading the wrong Macdonald. But who knows? Maybe that works for you these days, since Travis McGee's just another water rat who stands for nothing. Just like somebody else I know."

"And Detective Hunter?"

"Oh, some other actor," she explained, as if it was obvious, "I paid him two hundred dollars, and he had to practice his lines about ten thousand times before he finally got them right."

"So Violet's fine?" Eric checked.

"Of course," Irene snapped, bored with all the details. "Her sister was just a name in the newspapers."

Then, rather suddenly, Irene's resolve seemed to weaken, and she even lowered her weapon.

"Why'd you do it, Eric? Why'd you hurt me? I loved you so much. More than anyone else ever could or would, and you knew it, and you wrecked everything."

"I guess I didn't want a wife who might end up pointing a gun at me someday."

She looked at him coldly.

"Yes, you were *always* very clever, weren't you, Eric? But not quite clever enough to tell a decent story. But I could have helped you with that, and I could have been a good wife, and I could have learned to control my temper."

Then Irene sobbed a little bit, and her right hand lowered even further, and her Colt was now pointing at the floor. Eric had no doubt about the validity of Irene's grief, but he also knew that she was giving him a chance to pick up his Ruger.

But he didn't.

Eventually, Irene got control of herself, and she lifted up the Colt again and pointed it at his face.

"You know what they say in the mysteries, Eric?"

"What?"

"'If *I* can't have you, then nobody will.' I've tried for three years to get over it, but it's not going to work, and I knew it the day I left California, so now I'm going to blow your brains out."

"I don't think so," Eric said.

Which was clearly a "plot point" of some kind.

Despite everything that Eric knew and surmised about Irene's violent past, he still believed that she would never actually kill him. It was the kind of risk that he never took in life, and that he probably shouldn't be taking right now, but, whatever was about to happen, it was *his* plot now, and he was "writing" his own ending.

Irene fired the Colt twice, which sent two sharp echoes throughout the house after striking the wall behind the couch.

She'd fired high.

Intentionally.

"I know why you're here," Eric said, amazed at his own clarity, even tranquility, "and I know what you want, but I'm not going to do it."

"Pick up that gun, you bastard," she said, enraged.

But Eric didn't make a move. He didn't even look down at his Ruger, so she taunted him:

"You're such a coward!"

But Eric ignored her, and she seemed baffled.

"How did you kill her?" he asked, almost gently.

Oddly, Irene didn't seem to mind the question, and she answered immediately, without reflection, without equivocation.

"I pushed her off the back of the boat into the propeller," she explained, with unsettling composure.

"And that's why your mother left?"

Irene shrugged.

"I guess so. I guess she knew. I think she figured it out, but she didn't have any proof, so she ran away."

Eric had surmised as much. Then he asked what was, for him, the most important question of all.

"Why did you kill your sister, Irene?"

"Because it would make my life easier," she said without the slightest hesitation, without the slightest remorse.

"Did it?"

"Yes."

Which she said with remarkable conviction. As if she'd been tired of sharing her life with a duplicate and that whatever the negative ramifications of killing one's own twin sister might have been, she still felt that it was worth it, or that, at the very least, it was an acceptable trade-off.

"Drop the gun!"

It was Jane's police voice.

Jane was now standing in the doorway, and her weapon was pointed at Irene's head.

Irene glanced over at the door, obviously unimpressed.

"Oh, you go to hell, Jane!"

When Irene turned back to Eric, the shots rang out, sounding, this time, more like thick hollowish thumps since they'd hit both of their intended targets. Eric was hit in the thigh, what the pulp writers often call a "flesh wound," still believing that she wouldn't kill him and that she'd readjusted her aim at the last second. Simultaneously, Jane had blown a hole through Irene's wrist, and Irene, stunned and silent, slowly sank down into a chair and dropped her gun as two LAPD cops rushed into the room and took control of things.

Then Jane looked down at her brother, who was pressing

on his wound.

"You ok?"

"Yeah."

She believed him.

"So what did she want?"

> *7. Then he waits for his ex-fiancée who arrives with a*
> *weapon.*

"She wanted me to kill her."

In a bit of a blur, and quite efficiently, the paramedics patched up Eric's thigh and wrapped up Irene's wrist. Then someone rattled off Miranda, and, in no time at all, the cops had Irene heading for the door. But she stopped. She looked back at Eric, and, with her left hand, dropped a note to the floor.

Jane picked it up.

Then Irene was gone, and Eric felt sorry for her.

Before leaving for the hospital, he opened up the envelope and read the "outline," giving particular attention to the ending:

> *8. Having read the "outline," he realizes that his ex-fiancée*
> *wants him to kill her—for a number of reasons, including*
> *the guilt she feels about what happened to her twin sister*
> *when they were children, and also in an attempt to make*
> *him feel guilty for the rest of his life about killing her. In*
> *the better version, he realizes all of these things, and he kills*
> *her, thus ending his problems and hers as well, since he's too*
> *shallow to feel any guilt. In the weaker version, he contacts*
> *the police who arrive in time to apprehend his ex-fiancée,*
> *leaving the both of them messed up for the rest of their lives.*
> *(This, incidentally, is the cowardly version, and, thus, the*
> *more likely version.)*

"You know what I think?" Jane said later, at the hospital, ready to offer up another of her "theories." "I think that all of this insanity is about you giving up on being a writer. I think she was trying to make you realize, along with a lot of other deranged crap, that you need to work harder and not give up. Hell, maybe she was even saying, 'Write up *this* story. It might not be *Oedipus Rex,* but it's a start."

Eric looked up at his sister.

"So what are you? The literary detective?"

Jane smiled, and she left the room.

Then Eric read Irene's note:

> *Darling—If you did it, I forgive you, and I'm even grateful. If you didn't, which I fully expect, I can still help you. My poor distracted head is a claustrophobic labyrinth of stories and plots and striking incidents, and I'll send you more outlines from the penitentiary or the nuthouse or wherever they send me. Love, Irene*

NEW YORK CITY
(AND ENVIRONS)

The Plagiarist

A well-cultivated mind is, so to speak, made up of all
the minds of preceding ages; it is only one single mind
which has been educated during all this time.

— Bernard Le Bovier de Fontenelle

IT WAS THE DARK, AUSTERE, but sacred refuge of our young
lives—and we would move slowly within its rare sunlight
and gnostic shadows, beneath the dark paneled mahogany
walls and ceilings, down the endless exacting corridors of wooden
shelves, and under the portentous, crushing, yet exhilarating
erudition of the world's great volumes. Book after book, folio upon
folio, relentless, leather-bound, gilt-edged series after series—all
the comprehensive self-reflection of the provocative minds of
man waiting silently, in patience, that they might again reveal
what they alone contained. The Church Fathers, the Athenians,
the Germans, the Russian novelists, the British and Asian poets,
everything seemed represented and had its appropriate place, with
the somewhat eccentric exclusion of the French. There was, it's
true, a single copy of *Madame Bovary*, but having read the first
half, Father had concluded with rare generalization and chauvinism

that he saw no further reason to expend valuable shelf space on uninspired French exhibitionism. And, most amazingly, virtually all of the countless pages had been cut, because our father, a sincere and never ostentatious man, spent his entire life slowly but relentlessly learning what he might of man's accomplishment, and he'd spent his last, retired, and solitary years virtually confined to the library wing of the house in relaxed but considered perusal of his extensive collection.

But I begin in the library not merely for its symbolic significance in the tragedy of my older brother, Andrew, but in order to recall a seemingly insignificant incident that now seems to indicate the true depth and extent of his underlying problem. It was some dateless, distant, late October evening on the North Shore, and, as our father entertained a few guests at the east end of the library, we children sought out our most favorite and darkest corner that we might, in quiet seclusion, frighten each other with our most "horrible" stories. So we settled in that particular corner of the library where the best of the British authors seemed to converge—all the striking, handsome sets of Dryden, Pope, and Spenser; Shelley, Swift, and Goldsmith. As we took our seats on the cool wooden floor in the dark quiet recess, Andrew, the oldest of the four—about twelve years old at the time—noted with ominous effect that the Gothics were also shelved immediately above us: Walpole, Lewis, and Radcliffe; Poe and the Brontës. In such auspicious company, we soon began taking our turns, attempting to terrify the others, generally telling familiar stories of ghosts and demons and vampires. Finally, it was Andrew's turn, and we all waited with the greatest expectation since he was always the most effective—being already a voracious reader with a remarkable understanding of the eccentricities of Poe,

Hawthorne, and Gogol.

We were not disappointed.

He told a tale of a man named David Lang, a farmer not far from Nashville, who in the fall of 1880, in clear sight of his wife, his two children, his physician, and his best friend, vanished from the face of the earth in the low-cut pasture that lay before his home. His wife screamed and grew hysterical, the children were traumatized, and the men rushed to the exact spot of the incident but found nothing. For several days after, the neighbors searched the pasture but to no result, and, in time, although there was never a funeral, hope was gradually abandoned. Then, one rather ordinary evening, nearly seven months later, Lang's two children were playing in the pasture near the place of his disappearance, when his eleven-year-old daughter, suddenly sensing a peculiar presence, called out to her missing father. To their frightful astonishment, the children then heard the distant voice of their father calling out for help, over and over, until it finally faded away, forever.

It's hard to relay the chilling impact that this story had on the rest of us, although the fact that I can still, after all these years, recall its particulars so accurately might indicate the depth of its impression. We'd all, in fact, grown so fearful and uncomfortable at the conclusion of Andrew's story that we immediately returned to the east end of the library for the reassuring presence of the adults. Nonetheless, in time, we overcame our fears and became just children again, and we even discussed the story and its meanings at great length. Eventually, our young cousin, Kathleen, with the intention of praising Andrew's rendition, mentioned that the story seemed to have an especially terrifying effect because of its "familiarity." But this particular remark clearly stunned my brother who, with a certain animosity, looked challengingly at our young cousin, who innocently responded, "But, I've heard it before, Andrew." Actually, I myself was of the very same opinion, and I likewise felt that it in no way denigrated my brother's performance, but Andrew responded quite differently. He turned on little Kathleen, and with a frightening coldness and finality replied, "That is impossible, as I've made it up."

★ ★ ★

NEARLY FIFTEEN YEARS LATER, I received a brief note from my brother relaying the exciting news that his first two efforts at short fiction had been taken for publication by one of the more prestigious of the literary journals. At the time, I was working long hours in New York as a resident at St. Michael's, specializing in cardiology, and even finding some time for related research at Sloan-Kettering. I was living on the Upper West Side, working frantically but with a clear purpose, and somehow, finding time for my understanding fiancée, Jennifer. As a result, I'd seldom seen Andrew since his initial return from his year abroad in Europe and Asia Minor, spent mostly in Greece. As for Andrew, he was similarly preoccupied, having returned from Europe confident that the necessary groundwork for his literary endeavors had been completed. At the age of twenty-eight, possessing a remarkable erudition, and with three literary degrees (the most recent at Cornell), he'd returned to the old house in Huntington on the Island's North Shore to begin his life's work. He immediately began devoting his entire days to that end, and he was spared the harassment of financial concerns since the estate of our late parents had left us both financially independent.

Ever since those early days in the library, everyone had

confidently assumed that it was Andrew's inevitable destiny to contribute significantly to the literary annals. His natural modesty did not belie his determination, and his entire life had been one of preparation and dedication. He was disciplined, conscientious, even exacting, and his extraordinary breadth of knowledge was the result of a most serious scholarship. He had an admirable obsession with the absorption of knowledge, and he was able to fractionate and dissect every idea and experience with the most comprehensive rigidity. As a result, he set for himself the most rigorous standards and was, in essence, a perfectionist. It was an approach to one's vocation with which I certainly sympathized, since, to a certain extent, we shared many of the same characteristics, and, despite our divergent intellectual pursuits, we'd always maintained a close, congenial, and supportive relationship. So I worked on in New York City, and, during those first six months since his return from Europe, Andrew had worked relentlessly at his fictions. After his two acceptances, we met downtown for dinner, and we took satisfied stock of ourselves at the advent of our young careers.

But the problems began with the appearance of the subsequent issue following Andrew's two publications. I first discovered it during a late-night break at the research center, and I was shocked to see that the first ten pages of the issue were dedicated to a "special section" of letters to the editor making the most vitriolic and condemnatory charges of plagiarism against Andrew's work. Reading the first few letters, I assumed their authors to be rather shallow pedants ignorantly mistaking homage or allusion for literary theft. But as I continued reading, each attack grew more harsh and convincing, and all the letters cited definite yet generally different examples, including word-for-word borrowings from James, Poe, Hardy, Burke, Lawrence, Disraeli, Cooper, and countless others. The weight of the evidence was conclusive and damning. Finally, the "special section" ended with the editor's two-page response in which he apologized to his readers for his oversights, and then coolly disclaimed the author as a "fraud."

The first of Andrew's pieces, "Stonehenge," told the story of a disillusioned, lonely, American academic, Richard Ford, who receives a mysterious, scented, blank stationery-note postmarked "Bristol Downs," and then recalls a vow he'd made with a young English girlfriend during his undergraduate days at Cambridge ten years earlier. Impulsively, he sets sail for England—determined to appear at Stonehenge, exactly as they'd planned, during the rare convergence of the winter solstice and the lunar eclipse. When he finally arrives, he discovers her abandoned and dead, stretched out across the ruins' famous "altar" stone. The story's subsequent and rapid conclusion reveals the cause of her death, Ford's inadvertent involvement, and several startling repercussions. Though somewhat traditional in tone, the story was, at first reading, absolutely fascinating, and, even after the revelations, Andrew's ability to effortlessly absorb so many divergent writings within the dominant mood and style of his fiction seemed to display a virtuoso command of the language. For example, in an appropriately stiff correspondence to his cousin, Ford describes the ruin:

> . . . an assemblage of upright and prostrate stones on Salisbury plain, generally supposed to be the remains of an ancient Druidical temple. Given its singularity, and the mystery attending its origin, it's always necessary to view the ruins with an artist's eye—and contemplated by an intellect stored with antiquarian and historical knowledge.

The passage, so characteristic of Ford's shallow pedantry, is lifted virtually word for word from a little-known article of Poe's, "Some Account of Stonehenge."

The second story, "The Watching," told the bizarre case of a young attorney, who on the eve of his marriage suddenly vanishes, only to take up surreptitious lodgings in a nearby apartment from which he keeps his fiancée under constant surveillance. He continues to do so for over twenty years, even moving when the girl subsequently marries one of his former friends. When the friend is accidentally killed, the attorney finally and impulsively turns up at her door, consoles her, and is soon married. The obvious plot similarities to Hawthorne's "Wakefield" were minor compared to the varied borrowings from Emerson, Thackeray, Dostoyevsky, and even Thomas and Rilke. Once again, Andrew's capacity for the seamless absorption of disparate writings was absolutely confounding. At one point in the story, the attorney attends a religious service to observe his former fiancée and her family. The sermon, making a military analogy, emphasizes responsibility and free will, and, with the exception of a word or two, was taken intact from Disraeli's panegyric on the death of Wellington:

> . . . for the general must not only think, but think with the rapidity of lightning; for on a moment more or less depends the fate of a most beautiful combination—and a moment more or less is a question of glory or shame. All this may be done in an ordinary life, but to do all this with integrity is sublime.

The next day, I left the hospital early and drove out to the old estate. The house itself was empty, but, eventually, I found Andrew standing alone in the twilight looking out over the day's last reflections and shadows as they slowly shifted across the surface of the northwest pond. As I approached, he made no acknowledgement, so we stood together in the silence watching the geese slowly glide over the gradually darkening waters. I felt certain that he was suffering inside, but, as always, he was clearly in control of his emotions. Finally, he turned and looked into my eyes with a certain aggression.

"It's *not* true."

Naturally, having seen the irrefutable evidence, I was quite uncertain how to respond to such a brazen self-vindication, but Andrew continued, quite casually:

"You know, Matthews once wrote that 'frequent charges of plagiarism are a sign of defective education and defective intelligence.'"

Again, I made no response, and he turned away. Naturally, I wondered if such an esoteric citation had merely conjured up from his vast erudition, or whether it indicated a much more recent interest in the subject. I also took careful notice of his exact attribution of the quotation to its original source. As we slowly walked back to the house, I decided it best to finally confront the issue.

"Andrew, I want you to know that I've come to support you through all this, but I *have* read the charges."

Andrew stopped, and he faced me directly. His manner was firm and a bit condescending, but without any real malice. As he spoke, the sunset intermittently flashed into my eyes from over his shoulders.

"It's simply not true, and I have absolutely no intention of discussing it."

Since I had no desire to further upset my brother, there was an obvious and awkward silence between us. Then, as if to placate my concerns, he remarked rather off-handedly:

"Besides, I'm taking precautions."

Then we walked up to the house, spent a pleasant evening together, and never again broached the subject. I did, of course, remain quite concerned about his odd behavior, but he'd always been, just like father, a bit eccentric, and his comment about "precautions" seemed to at once acknowledge the problem and to make it clear that it wouldn't happen again. Later, as I drove back over the Island bridges into the soft-blue Manhattan night-lights, I felt a certain confidence about the problem itself, but I did wonder if the incident indicated something less than the capacity for literary genius which we had always assumed, without reservation, that he possessed.

The next four months were among the most hectic of my life. Not only were our medical researches reaching a culmination, but I also undertook increased responsibility at the hospital, as well as the most elaborate wedding preparations. Andrew was equally distracted, having resumed writing with an obsessive detachment. He confined himself to the estate, broke off his relations with a long-standing girlfriend, and generally avoided any form of outside communication. During these months, I only saw him once, on the occasion of his twenty-ninth birthday, when I drove out to the Island with a special birthday gift: a rare volume of Cooper, which I was certain was not contained in the family library.

Entering the house, I was disconcerted to notice that the library was padlocked, but when I eventually found Andrew in his large study, I was encouraged to see him looking so well, and I, again, marveled at our similar abilities to tolerate sleeplessness and overwork. Andrew seemed quite pleased to see me, and he admitted that his new work was going very well. But when I offered him my present, I noticed a certain hesitancy. Finally, he took the book, removed the wrapping with a certain unintended disinterest, read the title, and thanked me warmly.

"Do you have it?" I asked.

He looked at me for a moment, deliberated, and then chose to answer honestly.

"I've given up reading. I even reread only infrequently."

Seeing my disbelief, he added quite seriously:

"It only causes me problems."

After this direct yet rather casual reference to the plagiarism problem, his mood immediately lightened, he held up the book, and said:

"Maybe, someday!"

Andrew and I had always enjoyed each other's company, and that evening was no exception. He asked, with real interest, about Jennifer and our plans, and he also showed a genuine curiosity about the possible ramifications of my medical researches. He even offered to discuss his work in progress, a short novella based on the real-life experiences of James Mellaart, Assistant Director of the British Institute of Archaeology in Ankara, whose personal tribulations began on a train from Istanbul, when he noticed a young girl in his compartment wearing a priceless, solid-gold bracelet of ancient origin. When he questioned the girl, she casually told him that it was part of a larger collection found amid the ruins at Dorak during the Greek occupation after the First World War.

Impulsively altering his plans, Mellaart disembarked at Izmir and followed the young girl to her home where he found an astonishing collection of bronze-age relics that dated from

4,500 years old and rivaled Troy in consummate craftsmanship. Exhilarated, Mellaart immediately returned to the Institute and published his extraordinary findings, but when he was challenged, he quietly discovered that he was unable to re-locate the young girl. She seemed to have disappeared. Her address proved to be nonexistent, and Mellaart was unable to retrace his steps through the winding streets of Izmir. As a result, his highly regarded reputation was irrevocably destroyed, and speculation abounded—that he'd simply perpetrated a fraud, that he'd been deceived by jealous professional rivals, or that he'd been duped by an international smuggling ring which had "set up" Mellaart's article to increase the black-market sales of their contraband artifacts.

The story was absolutely fascinating, and I was very hopeful, especially when Andrew made it clear that although the fiction was based on a factual incident, it was most "original." I left that evening feeling reassured, and two months later when a note arrived mentioning that the book had been purchased by one of the more prestigious university presses, I was elated.

Archaeologist appeared in the fall of that year under a pen name, and within weeks was the obsession of the literary journals. Andrew's literary theft had accelerated to such an inconceivable degree that the book was a virtual compendium of Western literary achievement. The critics outdid themselves citing the plagiaries, and the book probably would have attained best-seller status had not the publisher, displaying an unusual integrity, chosen to withdraw the book and destroy the first printing.

It would be ludicrous to cite all of the original sources, but the range was absolutely extraordinary: Ibsen, Mann, Turgenev, Dickens, Malory, Tertullian, C.S. Lewis, Brockden Brown,

Trollope, and countless others. It seemed that there was not a single line of the book that didn't have another literary source, but once again, Andrew's ability to absorb these disparate pieces into a seamless stylistic continuity was truly uncanny, and even one of his most virulent detractors admitted that such "a dexterous plagiarist may do anything." Two examples will suffice. The first occurs as the archeologist is sailing northwest through the Saronic Gulf:

> Returning out of Asia, I sailed from Aegina towards Megara, and began to consider the country around me. Aegina was behind me, Megara was before, Pyraeus on the right hand, Corinth on the left. All these ancient capitals now pathetically prostrate over the rolling earth. And I wondered to myself, how can a man grow so disconsolate over his own meager trials, in the presence of such ravaged antiquity?

This passage from *Tristram Shady* recalls the most curious of all the book's plagiarisms, another "borrowing" from Sterne:

> Shall we forever make new books, as apothecaries make new mixtures, by simply pouring out of one vessel into another—as the ancient Romans robbed all the cities of the world to set their own sterile plot?

Andrew's breakdown was immediate, and my own inability, as a medical man, to properly foresee it, increased my own overwhelming feelings of guilt. The wedding was postponed, I took a leave of absence, and I spent two months at the estate. Andrew had totally withdrawn, and he refused any efforts at communication. He spent his days sitting in a chair on the veranda watching with seeming incomprehension as the wind fluttered the last of the autumn leaves. In time, however, there was a marked improvement, although he still refused to discuss the problem or make admission. He also refused any psychological therapy, most vehemently the Freudian type—a position with which I fully sympathized. Finally, we both agreed on an extended rest-vacation at a sanatorium in the Adirondacks. Andrew's progress in the mountains was quite rapid, and, within two months, he was back at the estate. We hired an elderly domestic to cater to his needs, and by the time of my wedding the following spring, he was able to stand as best man, although he chose not to attend the reception.

Naturally, I undertook an immediate and concentrated study of the problem, but I was very disappointed to find only the most cursory acknowledgements of the illness in the medical journals. I did, however, read all of the literary considerations: *Plagiarism* by Lindey, Paull's *Literary Ethics,* White's apologia for the Elizabethans, Edward's volume, and even Salzman's rather pedestrian discussion. It was all quite incredible for the layman, an admitted dilettante, to discover the truth of the notion that the history of plagiarism is indeed the history of literature, and the accuracy of Byron's contention that "the most original writers are the greatest thieves." Rare is the significant writer who has not been charged or caught at plagiarism, and the list is so extensive as to be almost inclusive. The mighty names of Demosthenes, Virgil, Shakespeare, and Byron are a disconcerting and instructive sampling. It soon became clear, as I studied further, that every language and every era had its plagiarists, and that the French seemed to have had a particularly distinguished tradition: Molière, Montaigne, Chateaubriand, Dumas, Stendhal, etc. The Count de Maubec even had the audacity to enumerate "Seven Rules for the Concealment of Plagiarism," and the aptly named Sieur de Richesource wrote a sixty-four page tract, *Le Masque des orateurs*, adroitly detailing the art of *"Plagianisme."*

But the French were hardly unique; both Milton ("Borrowing without beautifying is a plagiary") and Emerson found it justified if the original was improved upon, and, of course, Eliot went so far as to conclude that "Immature poets imitate; mature poets steal." There was even a time, I must admit, when I hopefully wondered if Andrew had simply developed a new literary form or style—that of using only what had already been written and coalescing all such disparate passages into a unique and superior original. Eight of the last lines of *The Waste Land* were "borrowed," but, of course, Eliot's purpose was different and the sources of his citations eventually noted. I was soon forced to abandon this last unlikely hope of literary justification, and I was forced to face the obvious fact of Andrew's mental illness.

Since there was no possibility that his countless "parallel passages" could have gone undetected, it seemed clear that Andrew's thefts were somehow both unintentional and unconscious, and that his plagiary was some deep-rooted and uncontrollable mental sickness. From a clinical point of view, I was well aware of the studies on compulsives, and though I refused to regard the plight of my brother from the narrow vantage of just another case study, several subsequent behavioral oddities only reinforced such an assessment. From his initial breakdown, Andrew had adamantly refused to take up his pen for any purpose whatsoever—even just signing his signature. I soon discovered that all writing implements had vanished from the house, and I noticed that the very appearance of my own fountain pen was a cause for anxiety, so I kept it concealed. Similarly, all reading materials were removed from the house at large and remained locked in the library. All of his numerous subscriptions were terminated, and his mail was left unattended. His phobia of books continued to increase, eventually extending to libraries and even to bookstores. On those rare occasions when we took a drive through the countryside, I fastidiously avoided the sight of any such establishments. These problems accelerated to such a phobic intensity that Andrew actually removed the portrait of our father from the living room, apparently because a small bookcase was vaguely visible in the distant background.

These exaggerated fears lasted for about four months during his initial convalescence, and, given his unstable condition, they seemed not unreasonable. But in time, Andrew gradually overcame these problems: the portrait reappeared, books were suddenly seen in his room, and, finally, a short note of gratitude arrived in the mail—apologizing for his "self-indulgence" and its "misfortunate consequences." He even wrote that, "The seduction of literary fame is a drug that dangerously stimulates one's vanity, and literary aspiration is, in truth, the great, characterizing, yet unacknowledged disease that stalks our desperate times."

Nevertheless, despite this most forthright and encouraging admission of his problem, I eventually became suspicious that Andrew was again reviving his dangerous interest in "writing," and, finally, one evening, when my concern had surfaced, we discussed it quite candidly. Andrew assured me that certain "unfortunate impulses" had made a literary career quite impossible, and he seemed sincerely determined to spend the next few years of his life adjusting to the situation, in pursuit of another vocation. Although I was certainly reassured, I still asked his kindly domestic,

Mrs. Winter, to keep a watchful eye—and over the next eight months, she observed nothing but a voracious reading from the now unlocked library.

In the meantime, my own life had somehow increased its pace: Jennifer had delivered a marvelous son, we'd purchased a home in northern New Jersey, my private practice had finally been established, and my continuing researches were beginning to produce notable results and attracting professional attention. Given what was to happen with Andrew, I now look back at that time in my life and continually ask myself if it would have been possible to do more than I did. I suppose it's always possible to do more for those who are the closest in our lives, but the extent of Andrew's relapse didn't become clear to me until one significant visit about two years after the initial collapse.

Arriving unannounced, I found him alone in the study reading, surrounded by literally thousands of books all stacked in neat piles and set on makeshift shelves. He looked worn and drawn, but his spirits were deceptively high. He answered my inquiries quite honestly, and I soon discovered that he had written another novel—an "apocalyptic" one—over a year ago. It was, he assured me, "entirely original," and, besides, he was "making sure." It was at this point that I discovered what still seems to me the most remarkable aspect of this entire series of unfortunate events: in order to be absolutely certain that he hadn't "borrowed" a single line or phrase from another author, he'd undertaken to reread *every* single book that he'd ever read! The audacity of this enterprise made me physically ill with concern, but Andrew felt that it was all quite reasonable. He'd gone into the library, removed every book which he'd previously read, and then begun a relentless rereading. He estimated the project at a year's duration (which seemed to me quite impossible), and now, being two months shy of completion—and "on schedule"—he was exhilarated to report that he had not come upon one single instance of "allusion" in his new novel.

That was the first time in our adulthood that I could recall raising my voice in Andrew's presence. He, however, remained most cordial and appreciative of my concerns, but he assured me that his problems were over, that hard work had been the best and only therapy, and that his life was now back on its corrective course. We parted amicably, but driving home I was tormented with the most cruel and perverse visions of his insane rereadings—sitting within that dark study, totally disconnected from any sense of reality, and surrounded by all those thousands of sinister and provocative books. I was totally distraught, and I felt utterly impotent. There seemed to be no satisfactory recourse. He'd adamantly refused to discuss any possibility of abandoning the project, and any thoughts of attempting to have him committed were also entirely unacceptable and might even, of course, exacerbate the problem. Naturally, I discussed all these terrible, mad, nerve-wracking anxieties with my wife and my colleagues, but I could find neither solace nor solution, and I braced for the worst.

Andrew's "novel" was accepted the following spring by a reputable publishing house, but, while it was still in galley proofs, the truth surfaced, and the project was scrapped. *The Camp of the Saints* turned out to be a word-for-word translation of Jean Raspail's visionary novel of the same title. The only reason that Andrew's deception had reached the galley-proof stage was that Raspail's novel, at that time, was still untranslated into English and was, as yet, only available in France in the French original.

Andrew's version ended with Raspail's frightening conclusion:

At midnight tonight her borders will be opened. Already, for these last few days, they've been practically unguarded. And I'm sitting here now, slowly repeating, over and over, these melancholy words of the old Prince Bibesco: "The fall of Constantinople is a personal misfortune that happened to all of us only last week."

I woke from the darkness when the police called and informed me that Andrew had taken his life with sleeping pills. I drove alone from New Jersey to the Island sick with grief, and guilt, and hopelessness. The house was in order, the terrified domestic sedated, and the library fully restocked. Andrew lay slumped over his desk, and the police left the room that I might read his note in solitude before the questioning.

No salutation:

> I could not continue in this state, either in the light of duty or of reason. My difficulty was that: I had been deceived greatly once; how could I be sure that I was not deceived again?
>
> I have not done that which is attributed to me. I have no knowledge of the individual Jean Raspail nor any facility with his language. These callous and relentless charges are unbearable. I feel certain I will go mad again. I feel that I can't go through another of those terrible times. So, finally, I am doing what seems the best.
>
> I must, however, despite it all, again affirm that literature and the creative effort have given me my greatest possible happiness.

★★★

M Y ONLY SOLACE in the subsequent months was that his pain and despair were over, and that whatever he'd done, he'd undertaken it without specific malice or intention. And all of these convictions were, once again, reaffirmed with force one rather pensive winter evening, many years later, which I passed in the quiet of the old library. I was casually browsing through an old, well-worn volume by Frank Edwards, when I inadvertently chanced upon the story of David Lang. Then, in the margin of the little book, I noticed the small, but telling, penciled checkmark in the unmistakable script of a child.

So I closed the book and recollected in the dark all of the vain and shadowy labyrinths of literary fame, and I remembered Edward Young's comment that, "So few are our originals, that if all other books were burnt, the lettered world would resemble some metropolis in flames, where a few incombustible buildings—a fortress, a temple, a tower—lift their heads in melancholy grandeur, amid the mighty ruin."

ELSEWHERE

Diploma Mill

FROM THE THIRD ROW OF THE KENNEDY CENTER, at the annual awards ceremony for the Modern Language Association, Shannon Moore paid absolutely no attention to the proceedings taking place before her on the stage. She was, instead, completely preoccupied by thoughts about her forthcoming flight to Athens, and by certain rather uncomfortable reminiscences of Professor David Burke.

She recalled a late afternoon in his temporary office several years ago. She remembered that the autumn twilight had gently settled into the room as they discussed various aspects of Ovid, particularly the fate of Phaëthon in Book II. She remembered that, at some point in the conversation, Burke had reached over to his desk for his concordance, and his eyes had accidentally, momentarily, fixed on hers—his own soft brown on her bright sea-green—and Shannon suddenly sensed, or seemed to sense, the same intensity of passion and longing that she herself had been feeling for well over a month.

Two weeks later, after the Classics Department picnic, it was dark and late on the university veranda. Almost everyone else had gone home, but the music was still playing. When a slow song, "In the Still of the Nite," a romantic ballad from the 1950s came over the speakers, Shannon asked Burke to dance, and she held out her arms. By that time, she'd had more than a few glasses of champagne, and she was very glad that she did. She felt, at that moment, that she truly loved David, and that he felt exactly the same about her. So now, as was perfectly clear to both of them, Shannon was offering herself without qualification, without compunction. She'd never done anything like it before in her life, but Burke just shook his head—not without some regret, she still liked to believe—and he said "I'm very sorry, Shannon," and then he went home to his wife.

She never saw him again, but maybe she would see him later today in Athens.

"The recipient of this year's Jean-Jacques Rousseau Award for Academic Integrity is Dr. Shannon Moore of UCLA."

As if from a great distance, Shannon heard her name announced, and it wasn't totally unexpected. Amid an enthusiastic applause, she rose up, went up to the stage, and took the wooden plaque from the MLA president.

She was being honored for her book, *The Insidious Mills: Diploma Mills and Their Damage to American Education and American Society.* The book had been published two years earlier, several months before she'd taken her current position as Assistant Professor of Education at UCLA. Almost immediately after its publication, the book had led to several FBI arrests for mail fraud, and a renewed and vigorous FTC enforcement of federal laws prohibiting deceptive commercial practices.

Shannon looked out at the huge crowd of university professors. She knew that she was a very attractive woman: tall, slender, with long brown hair and striking green eyes. She used to bask, rather self-indulgently, in the spotlight, but after all that had happened during the past two years, she had nothing to say.

"Thank you."

Then she left the stage, fully aware of everyone's disappointment, but she paid it no mind. She thought again of the Acropolis and imagined the deep and shimmering blueness of the Aegean.

Then she left the building.

From Union Station in downtown DC, she took the Amtrak north. She found a seat, off by herself, and she stared distractedly out of the window into the cold December afternoon. Everything had started right here, on this very same train, just two summers ago.

In the wake of all the media excitement about *Insidious Mills*—especially after the FBI arrests and her many subsequent talk show appearances—Shannon had been bombarded with letters and calls during her first year at UCLA. She certainly didn't mind the attention, and the following summer in DC, she chaired an NEH seminar on her specialty: college accreditation. She livened up the normally dull proceedings with special guests like Bernard Ramsdale, a convicted felon who'd opened at least sixteen different "universities"; Special Agent Owen Allister, the head of the FBI's Operation DipScam based in Charlottesville, Virginia; and Myron James, a man with sixty-six masters degrees and thirty-five PhDs.

The conference was a huge success, and, as a result, Shannon was awarded the American Council on Education's Exemplary Service Award.

But the night before the conference ended, she received a phone call at her hotel near Georgetown from a local entrepreneur named Jack Ramsey. He was quite upset that his younger sister had enrolled in "one of those sham universities." It was called the University of Athens, and his sister, barely eighteen years old, had already abandoned her studies at the University of Virginia.

Shannon was naturally intrigued. She'd never heard of this particular scam before, and she was also planning to write a short exposé about diploma mills with overseas connections. Since the girl, Rebecca Ramsey, would, apparently, never agree to a meeting with Shannon, it was finally decided that Shannon would approach her on the DC to Baltimore Amtrak which the girl rode every morning to work.

Back when Shannon was researching *Insidious Mills,* she'd done several stints of "undercover" work, usually on her own without FBI involvement, and she'd enjoyed playing "detective" very much. So tracking down Rebecca Ramsey seemed like just another useful adventure, and Shannon looked forward to it.

The next morning, she found the girl sitting alone in a pink and white dress in the third car of the Amtrak train, exactly where her brother had said she would be. The girl was reading a book, and Shannon sat down beside her. It seemed to be some kind of silly French romance novel, and Shannon was suddenly overwhelmed with pity for the poor girl. Was she really, as she seemed to be, some innocent young fool being duped by unscrupulous con artists? Or was it possible that she, herself, was devious and dishonest?

Shannon definitely suspected the former.

"So what are you reading?" she asked, breaking the silence.

The attractive young girl, who was both friendly and polite, actually seemed to appreciate the interruption.

"Something quite boring," she responded with a smile. "It's for school."

"What is it?"

"Émile."

But Shannon had already read the title off the cover.

"So what's it about?"

"Oh, it's a ridiculous book about education. I've never read so much nonsense in my whole life."

Shannon was naturally taken aback, and she glanced again at the cover of the book. Rousseau! Of course! She vaguely recalled that Rousseau had once expressed his theories about education in some kind of philosophical novel.

"He thinks that children," Rebecca continued, "shouldn't learn to read until they're twelve. And he thinks they shouldn't study any languages, or history, or literature, or geography."

Despite her obvious disgust, the young girl looked over at Shannon with another smile.

"Guess what he thinks they *should* do?"

Shannon was stunned by the question since she suddenly realized that she had absolutely no idea *what* Rousseau believed about education.

So the young girl gave the answer.

"Interact with nature."

Rebecca laughed a little bit, but she quickly caught herself. "I suppose it's not very funny. It's really rather tragic that the most famous book ever written about education, except for maybe *The Republic,* was written by a lousy tutor who'd abandoned all five of his children to the orphan asylum."

Then Rebecca looked directly at Shannon.

"Why is it that so many education 'experts' know nothing about children?"

Once again, Shannon had no response. She knew absolutely nothing about children, and she'd never read either *Émile* or *The*

Republic, and yet she was considered one of the most well-known educators in the country. She was also quite astonished by the direct and lively intelligence of the young girl sitting next to her. It was clear that Rebecca Ramsey was a remarkably well-read young woman, and, as their conversation continued, she casually quoted, without the slightest pretension, from Augustine and Chaucer and Swift.

Eventually, Shannon turned the conversation to the University of Athens, which Rebecca always referred to as her "correspondence college." She seemed perfectly pleased with her "studies," especially after a number of disillusioning experiences at the University of Virginia, and she hoped to complete her BA in about two years. She was also planning to take the related and "required" trips to Rome, Paris, London, and Jerusalem. She'd already gone to Greece several months ago, where she'd had a "fantastic" time, and Shannon could only imagine how much money the poor girl had already squandered.

When the train pulled into Baltimore, Rebecca rose up, said goodbye, and was gone. But Shannon stayed exactly where she was. She extended her ticket, rode all the way to New Hampshire, and then returned to DC on the same train. She spent the entire day and much of the early evening sitting in the same exact seat and thinking about a number of things.

But there were two things, in particular, that were on her mind. The first was her anger that this gentle, intelligent, young girl was being conned by some sleazy mill operator. But, of course, this was right up Shannon's alley, and she would take care of it. She would rip the "University of Athens" apart, and she would take great pleasure in doing so. But the second thing on Shannon's mind was much more disturbing. It was a persistent uneasiness about her own competence, rather, incompetence. How was it possible that a professor of education at UCLA, and the winner of the ACE award for Exemplary Service, had not read *Émile*—not to mention *The City of God, The Canterbury Tales,* and *Gulliver's Travels?* Shannon had no adequate response to these serious questions, and they troubled her deeply.

Surely her feelings had something to do with her persistent guilts about a certain type of laziness that had characterized much of her life. As a child, without trying very hard, Shannon had done quite well in her grammar and high schools in suburban Warrington, Pennsylvania—but never extraordinarily well. Nevertheless, early in her senior year, she was immediately accepted by the University of Pennsylvania, and when she suddenly found herself matriculated in an Ivy League school, everyone in Warrington knew why. At the age of fifteen, Shannon had written a short children's book based on the myth of Daphne and Apollo, and the book had been published, along with her mother's extraordinary illustrations, by Houghton Mifflin. Penn obviously saw her precociousness as a clear indication of her "potential," but she quickly bombed out of her classics courses, tried English for a while, and finally ended up as an education major.

And Shannon knew why.

She simply wouldn't work at the texts, and she always took the easy way out. At graduation, with rather unimpressive grades overall, but with A's in all of her education courses, she went to the University of Maryland. In less than five years, with a minimum of serious reading and a maximum of activity, she received her EdD and was already considered a national authority on accreditation. After all, she'd worked as an intern at the Council on Postsecondary Accreditation in DC; she'd finished

The Insidious Mills as her doctoral dissertation; and she'd become an expert advisor to the Department of Education's Eligibility and Agency Evaluation Staff.

During that time, Shannon, almost without realizing it, had undertaken a relentless campaign against all forms of non-traditional education, even various accredited programs run by respected universities through monitored correspondence, cable, or computer link-ups. She wasn't sure exactly why, but she found herself resenting any course of study that provided credit for "life" or "work" experience, or which eliminated residency requirements. Her increasing stridency had cost her some useful allies over the years, and, in time, even some friends. Even now, as a much-feted and highly respected academic celebrity, she felt strangely discontent, as if she really didn't deserve the adulation. She also seemed, in some inexplicable way, to actually distrust and resent herself.

Naturally, Shannon blamed much of this constant, yet subtly concealed internal anxiety on the emotional vacuity in her life. She'd never—and she could now finally admit it to herself—recovered from Burke's rejection, even though she was fully aware that if he *had* succumbed to her advances, she would have detested, and found untenable, the role of the "other" woman. As a result, Shannon had avoided all emotional attachments and involvements, despite the fact that men, of every type, found her very attractive and pursued her until it eventually proved useless. She was, she knew, a very lonely person. She was an only child, her mother was dead, and her father was living abroad. To deal with her persistent loneliness, Shannon always kept herself constantly busy, except for that day on the Amtrak train.

Yet nothing was resolved.

It was quite upsetting, and, in the end, Shannon did her best to push everything out of her mind. Even though Rebecca Ramsey had given her the US address of the University of Athens, she put it away and did nothing about it for over a year. She immediately returned to California and resumed her teaching responsibilities, but she was generally unmotivated, discontent, and atypically lethargic throughout the entire year. This debilitating sense of near-total enervation was further complicated by four other occurrences in her life that year.

The first took place in November, when her closest friend from Penn, Jane Arshen, committed suicide. Jane, within the previous six months, had not only lost her husband to a younger woman, but she'd also absorbed a blistering attack on her first book, *Multicultural Classroom Strategies and Teacherly Deconstructions*, because she hadn't used the most current forms of gender-inclusive language. It was sadly ironic that such a bright and progressive young woman should be abused for such a simple oversight. Naturally, Shannon was deeply affected by Jane's suicide, and she attended the funeral in Oklahoma City. But after the burial, she discovered, to her self-disgust, that she had absolutely nothing to say to the poor woman's devastated parents.

Then a few weeks later, one of Shannon's self-proclaimed "bitchy" rivals at UCLA, Diane Salis, claimed in a public forum that Shannon had only been hired because she was a woman. Shannon was absolutely stunned by the revelation, and she naturally refused to believe it. She believed, of course, in preferential hiring for others, but certainly not for herself. Surely, she tried to convince herself, she'd been hired on the basis of her own not-negligible merits. But Salis's cruel remarks haunted her every day—all day long—for over two months. Finally, late one night at the UCLA campus, Shannon surreptitiously examined the departmental files and pulled up the application letters. Salis was right. There was a candidate from Harvard named Stephan Clayton who'd applied for the exact same position which had been awarded to Shannon. At the time of his application, two years previous, Clayton was exactly the same age as Shannon, twenty-seven, but his record was far superior to hers in every way: grades, publications, quality of background, quality of recommendations, teaching experience, and everything else. Shannon closed the files and sat alone in the dark office for several hours trying not to think too much.

Then Shannon learned the fate of Gregory Scott, who'd been up for tenure in Shannon's first year at UCLA. Although, at the time, she couldn't actually vote, she'd lobbied very hard against him. Greg, as she knew, was a quiet, decent guy who went his own unobtrusive way, but he clearly lacked the innovative spirit that Shannon and others felt was necessary in the contemporary educational environment. Of course, it made no difference that he was an excellent teacher, or that he had solid publications. He simply wasn't the kind of "enthusiast" that the future of American education demanded.

After losing his job, Greg Scott, given his financial problems, had apparently lost his home as well. Unable to find another tenure-track position, he finally moved his family into the small farmhouse of his wife's parents in rural Vermont, and reliable rumors claimed that his depression was so severe that he might have to be institutionalized.

Then, at the beginning of the spring quarter, Shannon learned, for the first time, that Professor Burke's wife had succumbed to cancer three years earlier. Marie Susan Burke was generally known as an exceptional woman, being both intelligent and generous;

and it was also well-known, although Shannon had been in denial about it years ago, that she and her husband had a very close and loving relationship. Shannon had actually met the woman once, at a reception after a public lecture at Maryland, and she'd found the woman to be most charming, perceptive, and thoughtful.

But, now, the sudden and shocking realization that the woman was actually dead occasioned even more regrets and confusions in Shannon's disordered mind: regrets about her attempted seduction of the woman's husband; sorrow for the terrible loss that Burke had obviously suffered; and even a peculiar, yet undeniable, sense of further rejection since Burke had never contacted her, in any way, over the last three years.

Finally, more than a year after she'd met Rebecca Ramsey on the Amtrak train, Shannon sent away for a brochure from the University of Athens. As expected, it had most of the typical characteristics of the American diploma mill: no classes, no facilities, and no library; fees paid on a per-degree basis ($1,800 for the University of Athens's BA in Liberal Studies, though many "scholarships" were supposedly available); degree completion possible within two years; and a lack of accreditation by a COPA agency. The mill's stationery even carried the common and pretentious use of Latin on its masthead: *"Aut disce aut discede."*

Nevertheless, there was a curious admissions requirement: an exam supposedly based on the texts of two, terribly outdated, children's books known as *McGuffey's Eclectic Third* and *Fourth Readers*. Once accepted, students were also required to complete a "reading list," five exams, and five "intensive seminars"; and there was, apparently, no credit given for either past "life" experience or past "work" experience.

The University of Athens, like most contemporary diploma

mills, did its best to blur the distinction between itself and other legally legitimate and accredited non-traditional schools. Over the past decade or so, after the states had tightened up their regulations regarding degree-granting institutions, very few mills could simply "sell" diplomas like they did in the good old days when the notorious Alumni Arts, Inc., based in Oregon, sold 2,300 bogus diplomas in eighteen months for a very quick profit of over $100,000. When the proprietor of Alumni Arts was convicted and sent to jail, the other diploma mills suddenly got more "legitimate" by requiring some actual work, a few tests, telephone counseling, and, sometimes, even a few seminars conducted at a local motel. The University of Athens, though idiosyncratic in certain ways, clearly fit the current mold.

So Shannon enrolled.

She received her *McGuffey's Readers* (levels 3 and 4) in the mail, never bothered to open them, and took the entrance exam. It was administered by a local Los Angeles gardener, Alexis Garcia, a "graduate" of the University of Athens. Shannon took the test in a study room at the Santa Monica Library, and she failed miserably. It was a ridiculously hard test, full of difficult identifications, multiple choices, and matchings. The gardener did his best to be polite about it, and he even mentioned that he'd also failed the entrance exam the first time he took it.

Shannon said nothing, and she left the library. She was furious—although she wasn't exactly sure what she was furious about. She also felt humiliated. She immediately went back to her office at UCLA, picked up *McGuffey's Fourth Reader,* and began to read it. It turned out to be a rather amazing, quite challenging, and most enjoyable book of disparate readings, some by very well-known writers such as Milton, Johnson, Byron, and Irving, as well as many authors that Shannon had never heard of.

A month later, Shannon retook the test and passed, but just barely. Nevertheless, she was quite pleased, and so was Mr. Garcia. Now, he reminded her, she was ready to receive her first "reading list."

Part I of the "overall" list arrived two weeks later. Apparently, there were five separate reading lists, and there would be an exam and a seminar after each of the lists was completed. The student was allowed to read the works at his own pace, and eventually, after passing the exam for Part I, the student would go to Athens for an intensive five-day seminar. Of course, "scholarships" were supposedly available.

Shannon stared, somewhat blankly, at the list:

ANCIENT: Old Testament (selections), Iliad, Odyssey, Analects, Orestia, Antigone, Oedipus Rex, Trojan Women, Republic, Politics, Poetics, Aeneid, New Testament, Lives, Meditations, Discourse Against the Arians, On Illustrious Men, Confessions, City of God.

Had Alexis Garcia really read all these books? Had Rebecca Ramsey? Shannon doubted it very much.

She'd read one or two of these books in her past, and, without doing any further reading, she scheduled the Part I exam at the Santa Monica Library. Once again, her test was proctored by Mr. Garcia. Shannon read the first ten questions, feigned an illness, and left the library. It was definitely a "real" test, and she refused to get a zero.

That night, she began reading the books. It went quite slowly at first, and it was very difficult, but then she began to get more and more absorbed in the readings until, finally, she wanted to do nothing else with her time. She became, to her own astonishment, rather exuberant, and her intellectual life suddenly seemed exhilarating. She felt—she was fully aware—just like young Rebecca Ramsey.

Last month, Shannon had almost passed her second attempt at the exam, and she knew exactly why she failed—Aristotle and Athanasius had done her in. But now she was finally ready. She'd come to DC ostensibly for the MLA convention, but now she was taking the Amtrak north to Newark, New Jersey, where she'd retake the exam at an airport motel. If she passed, she'd fly to Athens later tonight.

But first, as planned, Shannon intended to make a quick stop in Princeton. She wanted to talk with David Burke and set a few things right.

It was four years ago that Professor Burke had come to Maryland for a year as a Distinguished Visiting Professor. Although he was only thirty-five at the time, Burke was already an internationally renowned classicist, and his recent translations of Marcus Aurelius were considered definitive. Originally from the Pacific Northwest, Burke had done his undergraduate work at St. John's in Annapolis and then completed his doctoral studies at St. Andrews in Scotland. By the time he arrived in Maryland, he was already a full Professor of Latin and Greek at Princeton University.

Shannon had signed up for his Latin poetry class, which was intended as a general education course for interested graduate students from all disciplines, with virtually all of the coursework done in English with translated texts. It was, without doubt, the best course that Shannon had ever taken in her life. It was full of Roman history, poetic eloquence, and philosophical depth. She loved the course, and she soon found herself also loving the teacher as well.

But, of course, things ended badly.

After the devastating incident at the Classics Department picnic, Shannon never saw Burke again. She was confused, embarrassed, and rejected, so she cut the last few classes of the semester and took an incomplete in the course. But before he returned to Princeton, Burke called her up on the phone. He was very polite and kind, and he sincerely wanted to help her remove the incomplete from her record. But Shannon was evasive, even unresponsive, and things were left up in the air. Then, the following semester, when Burke was back home at Princeton, Shannon persuaded another classics teacher, one with a justifiable reputation for slackness, to remove her incomplete. She did no further work for the class, even though she still owed Burke the final exam and a final paper. It was patently dishonest, and she knew it, but she did it anyway, and she tried to forget about it.

So today she would apologize for several things.

When the train arrived in Princeton, Shannon closed her Athanasius, and she walked over to the famous campus. Even in the winter, it was perfectly beautiful. She passed the McCarter Theatre, the Art Museum, historic Nassau Hall, and the Firestone Library.

When she arrived at the Classics Department, she learned from the secretary that Professor Burke, who'd resigned two years ago, about a year after the death of his wife, was also dead.

Overcome with weakness and with a bewildering combination of grief and shame, Shannon sat down unsteadily on one of the office chairs. In truth, she barely knew the man, yet he'd profoundly affected her subsequent life. Four years earlier, she'd come to believe that she truly loved what she'd so much admired—even admiring, in a strange way, his gentle rejection.

"Are you all right?"

Shannon could hear the secretary's concerned voice. Then she saw the glass of water.

Shannon nodded her thanks, sipped the cold water, and looked at the woman.

"When?"

"A few months ago."

"How did it happen?"

"It was a car accident. I'm very sorry."

She obviously meant it.

A car crash. It seemed a very odd way for a man like David Burke to die—so suddenly in such a tragically common way.

"Where?" she asked.

"I'm not sure. Probably in Washington." Then she added, "The state of Washington."

Shannon nodded once again, rose up, and walked to the door of the office.

"Are you sure you're all right?" the woman asked again.

"Yes, and thanks for your kindness."

Then, still quite numb, Shannon walked away to wander aimlessly down the department's corridors. At some point, it dawned on her that she might learn more from one of the other faculty members. Completely at random, when she saw the name "Alan Crane" on a partially opened door, she knocked.

"Come in."

Crane was a friendly, balding, bearded man. His bookshelves were full of the Greeks and the Latins, but he was reading something by Derrida, and he seemed very grateful for the interruption. Though he obviously had the greatest respect for his old colleague, he was also quite willing to say exactly what he thought about David Burke.

"At some point, he got very disillusioned," Crane explained. Then he looked over at Shannon with a smile, "It's easy to do."

"But why?"

"I'm not sure. He took Marie's death very hard. Maybe he just 'flipped out' a bit."

The man paused pensively, but Shannon tried to keep him talking, "What happened?"

"Strangely enough, he started getting involved in committee work." Crane seemed positively baffled by such a peculiar and distasteful idea, "It was something that he'd never done before, and I guess it shocked him quite a bit. He was always talking about 'corruption' and 'deception' and, to be honest, he got quite tiresome. He also began to let his work go—he'd been translating Cicero, as you probably know—and he wrote two rather unpleasant diatribes about academia, one for a low-brow journal and one for a very marginal one. Then he resigned."

Crane stopped, as if he felt that he'd already said too much.

"Where was the accident?" Shannon asked rather incoherently, as if it might, in some way, make a difference.

"I heard it was Washington State," Crane said gently.

Shannon stood up, thanked the man for his time, and went straight to the Firestone Library. She only had about an hour left, but she found the articles quickly, xeroxed them both, rushed back to the train station, and hopped on the express to Newark.

Determined not to dwell on Burke and his death and all her confusing, conflicting emotions, Shannon immediately pulled out her books and crammed the whole way to Newark. Two hours later, she walked into a small, empty conference room at the

Newark Airport Holiday Inn, and, somewhat nervously, took a seat and waited in the silence. Though Shannon felt reasonably confident, she never really cared for test taking and she'd already failed this particular exam twice before.

Then Rebecca Ramsey walked into the room. "It's good to see you again, Dr. Moore."

The young woman, just as she'd been two years ago, was perfectly polite. Since Shannon didn't know what to say, she said nothing.

Then Rebecca gave her the test and the instructions, and she immediately retreated to the back of the room and began reading from *The Collected Poems of W.B. Yeats.*

Shannon worked extremely hard, spending the maximum two hours on the exam. As she'd expected, it was a completely different test from the two she'd previously failed, but the questions covered the same material. When the time was up, Rebecca took the exam and left the room for about fifteen minutes. When she returned, she looked very pleased.

"Congratulations!"

Then she put the test on the desk in front of Shannon. The number "77" was marked in red across the top of the page. The passing grade was 70.

Then Rebecca spoke once again, with sincere admiration, "I only got 71 on this one. It's a *very* tough test."

Shannon nodded in agreement, although she didn't bother to point out that she'd received a 56 on her initial attempt, and 66 on her previous attempt.

Maybe the girl already knew.

But Rebecca was checking her watch. It was time to go.

"Have a great time in Athens, Dr. Moore."

Then the young girl smiled, handed Shannon a piece of paper, and started for the door.

Curious, Shannon called out after her, "Have you finished yet?"

"Not yet. I'm almost done with Part V."

Then Rebecca held up her collection of Yeats, "but I wish it would *never* end."

Once again, Shannon said nothing, and, as the young woman vanished through the door, she picked up the sheet of paper. It was the reading list for Part II:

> *MEDIEVAL AND RENAISSANCE: Beowulf, Summa Theologica (selections), Divine Comedy, Canterbury Tales, Imitation of Christ, The Prince, The Institutes, Spiritual Exercises, Dr. Faustus, Shakespeare (12 plays and the sonnets).*

Later that night, during her Olympic nonstop to Athens, Shannon flipped on the night-light above her and read Professor Burke's two articles. The first, entitled "Don't Send Your Children to College," was published in the February *Reader's Digest* almost two years ago. It was a very firm warning to parents about the severe problems involved with American education, and it suggested that most high school graduates would be far "better" and far "wiser" people *without* a college education.

The article was a provocative litany of concerns, statistics, and examples: pregnancy and abortions (one third of American abortions are performed on students), ideological indoctrination (regarding sex, the environment, population control, nuclear energy, capitalism, religion, the military, and so on), faddish emphases on peripheral studies (and the consequent rejection of the traditionally accepted core of classical texts), inadequate writing skills competency, exorbitant tuitions, grade inflation, exploitation of athletes, abuse of minority students through preferential placement/mismatching, and much more.

While admitting that a few students *could,* with proper advisement and careful course selection, achieve a decent education at certain schools, Burke emphasized that most students simply do not. Given this fact, the article stated, in no uncertain terms, that it was foolhardy for parents to spend huge amounts of money on a suspect education or, as Burke consistently termed it throughout the article, "miseducation." He also suggested that serious parents should read the various, well-known, recent studies on American education by Kirk, Bloom, D'Souza, Sowell, and others.

Then Shannon read the second article, "Academic Malfeasance," which was much more of a scholarly essay, appearing last winter in a rather obscure quarterly entitled *Crisis in Education.* The point of the essay was pretty much the same as the *Reader's Digest* piece, but it took more of an historical and theoretical approach. It focused on the writings of Rousseau; the "upcreep" of Parker and Dewey; the radicalism of the sixties, and the "increep" of Rogers and Maslow. It was thoroughly pessimistic, and it offered no possible hope of a revival for the moribund educational system.

When Shannon was done, she put the articles away and shut off her reading light. Everyone around her was sleeping in the quiet, high-altitude hum of their transatlantic night flight. Shannon knew nothing about Parker and Maslow and the rest of the theoreticians, but she did recognize everything that Burke had discussed in the *Reader's Digest* piece. Many of these very same problems had, on various occasions, bothered her over the years; nevertheless, she'd proceeded right through the entire system, absorbed all its beliefs and all its methodologies, and finally emerged as one of its staunchest defenders.

But Shannon was no longer complacent. Over the past several months, she'd learned just how poorly educated she really was. She'd been forced, for the first time in her life, to look at herself honestly, and to reevaluate the whole gigantic system that she was a part of. In the end, she'd come to see herself as not much better than a fraud, as someone who was poorly educated and who'd willingly and defiantly perpetuated an incompetent and corrupted teaching system. She now realized that her almost fanatical devotion to that system, which had expressed itself in her relentless attacks on not only the fraudulent diploma mills but on all of the non-traditional modes of higher education, was the result of her own intellectual insecurities and guilts and defective vanity. Even if Shannon wasn't quite ready, like Professor Burke, to indict the *entire* education system, she had to admit that American universities did much more indoctrinating than educating, and that the tangible results of a university education certainly couldn't justify its exorbitant costs.

Finally, just before Shannon fell off to sleep, she wondered what she was getting into tomorrow. If the University of Athens was some kind of elaborate con game, it certainly, at least so far, hadn't made any money off her matriculation. Just like young Rebecca Ramsey, Shannon had received a full academic scholarship, and they'd even paid for her plane ticket as part of some kind of "travel grant." Similarly, if the University of Athens was really an academic fraud, it had, nevertheless, taught Shannon more in the last few months than she'd learned in her eight previous years of university study.

Whatever the case, she'd enjoyed all the reading—all the various adventures of discovery and self-discovery—as well as her new sense of confidence. To her own astonishment, she'd enjoyed reading Plutarch's *Lives* much more than anything else in her whole life, and soon, due to the University of Athens, she would do something that she'd dreamed of as a child—stand on the Acropolis. As for whatever else might happen, she would deal with it as best she could tomorrow.

The next morning, Shannon disembarked at the Athens International Airport and took a taxi to Cape Sounion, southwest of the city and not far from the Temple of Poseidon, where her "intensive seminar" was to be conducted. She was driven to an isolated, white-stucco villa which overlooked the Saronic Gulf. It was endlessly blue and perfectly spectacular.

Leaving her bags in front of the house, Shannon walked around the back of the villa to look at the water. For a long time, she stood there alone, strangely content for the first time in many years, occasionally wondering who'd come up behind her—to welcome her to the University of Athens. Actually she'd thought about it quite a bit over the past few months, and, at times, she was more than willing to let her imagination get the better of her. Maybe, she wondered, it would be Stephan Clayton, the man who'd applied for her teaching position at UCLA. Or maybe it would be Gregory Scott, the man whose tenure she'd sabotaged. Or maybe it would be Jack Ramsey, the concerned brother of young Rebecca who'd first called her about the University of Athens. Or maybe it would be some vengeful diploma mill operator who'd been imprisoned because of her book.

Or maybe it would be David Burke, the brilliant Classics professor whom she'd once believed she loved. He would come up behind her and say, softly, with a smile, "So, Shannon, you've finally come to finish your incomplete?" and Shannon would turn around and say, though it was obvious, "You're not dead, David?" and he would smile again and say, "Let's take a walk on the beach," and she would say, "But what if we fall in love?" and he would smile and say, "So what if we do?"

Naturally, this was Shannon's most favorite unlikely scenario, one that she'd conjured, with the greatest pleasure, early this morning in a comfortable half-sleep, as the 747 glided into Greece. And now, fully awake, high above the Saronic Gulf, she could laugh at herself a bit, even though she still saw nothing at all pathetic in her rather absurd fantasies. Because some things, some truly powerful things, really do die hard.

Then she saw the marker, and she walked closer.

It was a waist-high, cut-marble stone with a small bronze plate, classic but unobtrusive. It was engraved as a simple "In Memoriam" dedicated to "David Edward Burke" and "Marie Susan Burke" from the University of Athens. It also listed their dates, and Burke had obviously died, just as they'd told her at Princeton, a few months ago.

Shannon had no further doubts about it, and she remained surprisingly calm. There would be no debilitating weakness, and no sense of uncontrollable desperation.

Everything remained calm.

Eventually, Shannon turned around and walked back towards the house, into the bright Attic sun. As she did so, she could see a man sitting on top of the roof of the villa, dressed in a white suit. He'd probably been there the whole time, and he seemed to be, patiently, waiting for her to come and join him.

As soon as Shannon noticed the steps up to the roof, she

immediately went up, and the man rose to greet her.

"It's good to see you again, Shannon Moore," he said.

His light blue shirt was open at the collar, and his jet dark hair contrasted sharply with the whiteness of his suit. He was, she was surprised to notice for the first time, strikingly handsome.

It was Alexis Garcia.

"I thought you were a gardener?" she said with a certain mischievous amusement.

"I am," he responded. "Have a seat."

There was a second chair waiting on the roof, and they both sat down. Their much-extended view of the gulf was far more breathtaking than anything Shannon could have ever imagined, so they sat in the silence for a while until she finally asked Garcia about Burke.

"So he's really dead?"

"Yes," Garcia responded, "a car accident on Highway 12, not far from here."

It was really that simple, and it was all over, and Shannon decided not to ask anything more about it.

"And who are *you*, Mr. Garcia?"

"Professor Burke directed my dissertation at Princeton about six years ago. Then I taught for a few years, discovered that no one was really interested in the classics, so I bailed out. I returned to LA and worked with my cousin Carlos. It was what my family always called "honest" work, and, I must admit, I really enjoyed it. Then, after Burke had his "awakening," we hooked up again. As it turned out, I was actually the University of Athens' first student. And Jack Ramsey was the second."

Shannon thought it over for a few moments.

"So Burke *was* the University of Athens?"

"Yes."

"And now it's you?"

Garcia nodded.

"How did it happen?" Shannon wondered. "And why did Burke do it?"

"It was Mrs. Burke, Burke's wife, Marie, who forced him out of his scholarly slumbers. It began about three years ago, when she was dying with the cancer, and she decided to audit a class at the university on German history. Her parents had been immigrants from Bavaria, and she'd had a lifelong interest in the subject. But the course was a disaster. The Professor taught no *real* history at all, and his first six classes consisted primarily of enthusiastic ravings about the Baader-Meinhof gang. Fed up, Marie dropped the class, and she asked Burke to find out if "this kind of nonsense" was common at the university. If it was, she wanted him to do something about it. Which he did.

"Soon after her death, Burke began looking into it. He actually knew very little about American education, but he learned quickly. He joined several university committees, sat in on various classes, attended seminars, and fought in the battle over the core. All of his efforts were completely useless, so he got out. He resigned, wrote the article for *Reader's Digest,* dug up some money, and started the school. The response was overwhelming."

After a brief pause, Garcia continued, "He always hoped you'd come and help him out."

"Then why didn't he just call me?" Shannon asked with confusion, yet without bitterness.

"Because he was afraid that you wouldn't have come for the 'right reasons.'"

Shannon was amazed and even slightly shocked that Garcia

seemed to know so much, but, strangely, she didn't mind. Besides, she knew it was true, and now, ironically, when she was *finally* ready to help Burke, it was, of course, too late.

"I wanted to apologize for several things," she confided softly, almost to herself.

"The incomplete?" Garcia guessed.

He pulled out a sheet of paper from his jacket pocket, "We found this in his papers. It seems that you owe him a final paper and a final exam, and he still expected to get them both."

Astonished, Shannon looked down at Burke's "reminder" sheet. She was very pleased to see that all her previous grades in his course had been A's, and she remembered working, quite uncharacteristically, extremely hard in his Roman poetry class, until she suddenly dropped out.

"I've also found Burke's final exam from that semester," Garcia explained, "and I'd be glad to administer it."

Shannon was quite amused by his thoroughness, and grateful for his thoughtfulness.

"I bet you could grade the paper too?" she smiled, "Maybe something on Pindar?"

"I'll be glad to," he assured her.

Strangely, unexpectedly, Shannon was overcome with a powerful sense of relief and comfort.

Then she heard his voice again.

"*Then* maybe you'll help me out at the University of Athens?" Garcia added, rather cautiously.

"Not until I get my degree first!" Shannon laughed.

And Garcia laughed as well, for the first time. Then he pointed down at the water. "Would you like to take a walk on the beach?"

Shannon turned and looked at him directly, into his dark eyes.

"Yes, I would, very much."

For the next few hours, they walked up and down the coast and talked about Burke and Marie and the classics and diploma mills and many other things. Then later that same day, with two other students—a middle-aged secretary from New Jersey and a farm kid from Kansas—they went over to the Acropolis and their "intensive" seminar began. It focused primarily on Plato and Aristotle, and it was very intense.

So was Garcia.

Shroud

THESE PORTUGUESE TWILIGHTS FLUSHED THE INTERIOR ROOMS of the Royal Villa with a soft quiet light that fell gently over the ancient portraits of the House of Savoy, and then fell further away to the massive wooden doors of the study which slowly drew open for Umberto II, ex-King of Italy and present Count of Sarre. We embraced for the first time in these twenty-seven years since he'd flown to exile, flying from the Ciampino Airfield on the outskirts of Rome, for an overnight stop in Barcelona, before the present and voluntary exclusion on the Bay of Cascais.

We spoke warmly for nearly an hour, recalling the war, the Allied invasion, and the close friendship that had grown so quickly between a young Army Captain directly assigned by Eisenhower as military attaché to the Royal family, and the "heir apparent" and current Lieutenant General of the Realm. We discussed the liberation of Rome, our somewhat reckless reconnaissance flight over German lines, and the bitter aftermath of industrial stagnation, mass unemployment, famines, riots, the communist bid for power, and the extremely close national referendum on the monarchy. The King had apparently taken his seventy years of royalty, war, and seclusion well, and he spoke of his memoirs.

Later, when the sunlight's passing had slowly dimmed the room and the wine had passed from its decanters, there came between us a sudden and lingering silence, and I anticipated an explanation for his desperately urgent message of the previous afternoon that I stop in Cascais on the way to Turin and tomorrow's press conference—which was scheduled to precede both the preliminary and restricted viewing of the Shroud, and the subsequent and much-anticipated television exposition.

"The Redemptionists are fine soldiers, as we know, in a more important way." Then the King rose to leave, sorry that the time had come so soon, and that, again, there were things that were more than friendship. "And, yes, there's a matter that Guarino will relate, for your consideration. I wish you strength and pleasant flights." Then, at the door, he paused and turned. "This portrait at the window is Princess Clotilde, who mended, on her knees, the backing of the Shroud before the 1898 exposition."

The taxi flew lightly through the mild November night down the Corniche Road that leads to Lisbon and the mouth of the Tagus and away from the Boca do Inferno. The seawinds blew softly through the early dark as we drove down the lantern-lit beaches of the Costa do Sol.

Ninety-six years after its first appearance in Europe, the childless Margaret de Charny transferred the Holy Shroud, the burial shroud of Jesus Christ, to the pious Duke Louis of Savoy in 1453. Due to a damning but misinformed memorandum of Pierre d'Arcis, Bishop of Troyes, in 1389, the fourteen-foot linen, imperceptibly stained with a pure sepia monochrome image (front and back) of the crucified Christ, was generally considered a medieval artistic forgery until the vindications of modern science. Its permanent residence in Turin, since 1578, was disrupted during the war by Nazi curiosities and the fear of aerial bombardment, until it was then removed by Prince Umberto to a stone fortress overlooking Avellino, 140 miles south of Rome. After the German collapse, we escorted the Shroud back to its permanent residence in the Santa Sindone, Cathedral of St. John the Baptist, where its temporary curators, Benedictine monks, were rewarded with a private viewing. I was present that day, overcome in a manner frighteningly uncharacteristic, struck with the presence of something truly extraordinary in the midst of the war-torn continent, aware, as Paul Claudel, that "something so frightening and yet so beautiful lies in it, that man can only escape it by worship."

Even before the turning of the present century, at least twenty popes had specifically expressed a personal trust in the Shroud's authenticity. But it was to be in this tragic and beleaguered twentieth century that its time had come. Pope John XXIII perceived it as "the Lord's doing," and Pope Paul VI felt that it was "the most important relic in the history of Christianity." I, myself, given my present remove from the church, preferred to focus on the scientific and historical evidence, but, regardless, it was only a matter of education via the media which would thrust the Shroud into the very center of twentieth-century intellectual speculation. And tonight was the night of November 21, 1973, the eve of the Shroud's television exposition, over Eurovision, to an audience of 200 million Europeans and South Americans.

That contemporary scientific evidence had shifted the burden of proof back to the nonbelievers is generally accepted. Its authenticity is detailed in the studies of Walsh, Rinaldi, and my own recently completed manuscript, *The Authenticated Shroud,* considering: its inexplicable and exacting negative image discovered in 1898 by Secondo Pia; its anatomical flawlessness; its exactitude in the depiction of crucifixion, a form of execution terminated with Constantine and not fully understood until the Barbet experiments of the 1930s, i.e., that the nails passed through the space of Destot in the wrist and not through the palms; the Raes discovery of cottons in the linen (at the Ghent Institute of Textile Technology) of the species Gossypium herbaceum, indigenous only to the Middle East; the positive identification of Dead Sea halophyte pollen by Dr. Max Frei, Zurich biologist and criminologist; the exacting accordance with the scriptural recordings of the passion and death; the clear lack of pigment and brush strokes; and on and on.

Where science succeeds and continues to succeed, there now comes historical verification in the imminent reports of Ian Wilson, a young British historian up from Oxford, who has, with remarkable facility, been able to trace the Shroud, as delivered by the disciple Thaddeus, to Abgar V of Edessa, who died in 50 AD. During subsequent reigns and persecutions, the Shroud, also known as the "Image of Edessa" or the "Mandylion," went underground until its rediscovery in the sixth century. In 943, Emperor Romanus Lecapenus ordered his armies to Edessa to capture the Mandylion and return it to Constantinople where it remained until the Fourth Crusade's unpropitious sack of that great city in 1204. The Shroud then fell into the hands of the Knights Templar, who worshipped it at Acre, Cyprus, Marseilles, and finally Paris. When Philip the Fair destroyed the order in the fourteenth century, the Shroud was surreptitiously delivered to an heir of the martyred Templar, the Master of Normandy, Geoffrey de Charnay.

Out from Lisbon, the Portela Airport gently lit the dark skies to the northeast. Guarino, the King's retainer, had, as requested, rearranged my flight reservations, and after exchanging tickets and rechecking the status of my luggage, I retired to the airport chapel with a half an hour remaining to departure. The room was lonely, poorly lit, and somehow godless. I rested for a while and reaffirmed my purpose. Eventually, from total exhaustion, I regained my strength, and then silently removed the German Luger P-08 I'd confiscated at Tarquinio in 1945 from beneath my cassock and snapped the safety to check the barrel and clip.

The night flight flew over the dark peninsula eastward into the night before the coming day. Even with the exhaustion and preoccupations, I was willing to consider the pathetic irony of the present situation and my lifetime obsession with questions of ethical morality. At Dartmouth, just before the war, I'd written a dissertation on Clerical Morality, concocting a rigorously logical system of "Synoptical Ethics." It dealt, specifically, with the fate of heretics, concentrating on Arius, and posing the possibility that Motive, End, and Duty can actually justify the Means in peculiar cases of doctrinal matters. It found little favor in any quarter, and it was generally considered, by those who'd probably not bothered to read it with the prerequisite tenacity, a pedantic and unconvincing theological apologia for morally reprehensible acts.

After the war and joining the Congregation of the Most Holy Redeemer, I soon learned that such polemic was best avoided during my doctoral studies in Sacred Theology in which the focus fell on the final stages of St. Alphonsus Ligori's moderate moral system, Equiprobabilism, as found incomplete in the seventh edition of the *Theologia Moralis*. But in time, I discovered that I was unable to refrain from speaking my mind, and I was almost immediately rejected from the order as "heretical"—although one of the deciding traditionalist fathers would admit at the time, "nevertheless, a quite brilliant unorthodox." This was, of course, long before the remarkable "openness" of the spirit of Vatican II, which would have surely welcomed my disputations of various aspects of the magisterium.

Over the subsequent years, bitter and even somewhat ashamed, I'd never mentioned the Redemptionist's rejection of my apostolate to the exiled King in any of our limited correspondences. But now, having worn the clerical garb for his benefit, I reflected that it would also, ironically, facilitate my passage.

Throughout the gentle flight, I struggled for sleep, well aware that I desperately needed some rest for the coming hours, but an endless stream of the countless theological passages which I'd once studied in the seminary ripped like a series of sharp violent headaches through and beneath the depths of my eyes. Eventually, from somewhere within this confused, exhausted rush, there was a single, peculiar, and secular Argentine maxim that I could finally embrace: "Whosoever would undertake some atrocious enterprise should act as if it were already accomplished, should impose upon himself a future as irrevocable as the past."

The sun of the following day woke me to the landing at the Kalandia Airport. Grateful for the rest, I still felt a great disappointment in not having seen the ancient city from the morning skies. Rested, resolved, and yet disturbed at having come to Jerusalem without having seen either its splendor or its strength, I disembarked.

Two hours later in the arid rock desert near Qubeiba, I kicked open the front door to Weizman's secluded bungalow. He emerged from another room, and he approached me cautiously, uncertain.

"Richard Thompson? Is that *really* Richard Thompson? What incredible coincidence could possibly bring you to Qubeiba?"

"The Shroud discovery."

"But how could you know? I've only telegrammed Vercelli this morning." He seemed genuinely puzzled, not only by my sudden appearance, but by my attire as well, yet he remained strangely calm and unalarmed.

"Has anyone else been informed?" I asked.

"Not yet. It's to be announced at the press conference this evening."

"Is it here?"

"Yes, and I believe quite safe. Why, is there any danger?"

I removed the Luger from beneath my cassock and immediately fired through his forehead at point blank. He flew backwards over the desk, slumping to a rather pathetic position on the floor of the bungalow. There was certainly no need to fire again, and somehow, within myself, I found some pity for the man, and I believed that he'd died as quickly and painlessly as he might.

The smell of kerosene soon filled the cottage, and I kicked a cover over his face. Weizman was an Austrian Jew who took an atheist's perversion in impugning Christian beliefs and scripture. Nevertheless, his renowned reputation as an archeologist was certainly justified, as he'd worked Mesopotamia with Sir Leonard Woolley, and then, years later, assisted Kathleen Kenyon with her diggings in Jerusalem. Over the years, he'd also somehow managed to maintain a reputation for professional integrity despite his overt anti-Christianity. But where Savoy had only sensed the danger in his sources' report that a stunning Weizman discovery would be revealed at today's Turin press conference, the once-King would never have known that Weizman was also chief archeologist at a dig in Urfa on the eastern Anatolian steppeland of southeast Turkey.

And Urfa is Edessa.

So, now, I suppose, I should make an effort to explain my own speculations about the Weizman discovery. If we accept from the scientists, then the linen of the Shroud dated from antiquity, once held a true human corpse, and once held a corpse that had borne the exact scriptural wounds of Jesus Christ. The French Jesuit Paul de Gail once estimated that the odds of a similar crucifixion having occurred at that time are over 225 billion to one. If we also accept Wilson's history, then the Shroud is verifiable past Edessa. Generally, all the modern studies have emphasized either the Vignon vapor theory of image transferal or the flash photolysis proposed by the young Air Force Academy scientists, Jackson and Jumper. But it was always the original "contact" theory that had, for nearly thirty years, most concerned me in my various speculations regarding a possible scenario that might verify an inauthenticity.

If, during the Christian persecutions begun in Edessa under Ma'nu VI, consider and suppose the possibility that the original Shroud might have been destroyed, and, within the extreme perversities of that ruthless persecution, a Christian (or Christians) was subjugated to the exact same passions of Jesus Christ. Then the dead body might be subjected to bas-relief rubbings in the manner of the Chinese, dating from 200 BC, in linens coming, by perverse coincidence, in trade from Palestine. This subsequent artifact would have been used to blaspheme and vilify the captured Christians. Then, in the sixth century, when it was finally rediscovered, it would naturally be assumed to be the one, true, and holy Shroud. In all my twenty-seven years of Shroud study, this scenario had always remained my single most obsessive fear, and now, somewhere in this bungalow, Weizman had hidden the evidence.

Coming outside, in the raw red heat of Palestine, another intense wave of heat flashed up from behind me as the cottage ignited and exploded. I turned to watch the blaze as it fired up into the dry desert air, and I felt nothing but regret that Weizman's unfortunate telegram would now necessitate further and immediate action. Somewhat mesmerized, and fully aware of it, I stood and watched as the small house and Weizman and all his work were quickly consumed in the rising flames.

My nonstop flight left Israel for Rome at 9 AM, and I eventually arrived, on a connecting flight, in Turin at 10 AM, due to the time zones. Vercelli, I knew, would be staying at the rectory of the Church of the Consolata, and I recalled, as the taxi raced through the Turin Streets, how this simple harmless man had always shown me nothing but kindness. But time was running out, especially since Cardinal Pellegrino's initiating press conference was scheduled for noon at the Royal Palace.

When I finally arrived at the Consolata, it was with the greatest relief that I found the Monsignor, with his head bowed deep with prayer, alone in the rectory chapel holding the telegram in his right hand. When the silencer had been quickly screwed to the barrel, I lowered the gun, pointed to the back of his neck, and faltered. Suddenly, there occurred to me the terrifying possibility of killing this decent priest in a moment of despair, a horrifying presentiment. But then, with a startling abruptness, Vercelli turned and saw me, though not the Luger, with a shocking look of elation and an almost perverse and inexplicable satisfaction.

"Has anyone else read that telegram?" I asked.

"No. Has Weizman . . ."

The gun rose to his face, and it blew a hole high through the forehead between his eyes. He collapsed back over the pews, and the telegram floated gently to the floor at the aisle. Quickly, I retrieved the paper, replaced the Luger, and was, at once, safely to the streets and reading Weizman's message:

> Ledgers of Nicodemus, 37 AD, uncovered in NW Jerusalem. Describe S. in detail & trans. to Abgar at Edessa. Corroborates Wilson & verifies S. Please do not circulate until conf. Wedn. Sincere. Albert Weizman.

So I find myself writing this narrative over and over again, and in so many ways, each the truth. Yet each deposition, each confession, brings neither satisfaction nor retribution. With each passing day, as I hide these versions in the various books and places of my room, I find, upon awakening, that they've all been vanished, and I presume destroyed. So I continue to suffer as I deserve, greatly, and possibly as greatly as I can, but not nearly as much as I deserve.

All of those events, both Jerusalem and Turin, actually took place many years ago, before the great success of the television exposition and the "perfect curve" of the Jackson-Jumper microdensitometer correlating-graphs which seemed to finally negate the possibility of contact theories. Even the subsequent carbon-dating fiasco of 1988 has now, of course, been superseded by the labs' inexcusable ignorance of obvious contaminants, specifically "bioplastic" coating, and the withering skepticisms of Dr. Harry E. Grove, the founding father of the techniques of carbon dating.

So I now continue to live every single moment with the constant and revolting revelation of what I truly am: a frightfully shallow pedant who, like the most smug of the Pharisees, willfully abandoned the true meaning of his faith for fanatical devotion to an external manifestation, a possibly marvelous relic, which, whether authentic or not, should never have become the fundamental and motivating determinant in an individual's life: because a man with heretical beliefs cannot dance around the faith with a bizarre and groundless devotion to a possible sacramental, and because the incidentals of the faith have no real meaning without the gospel, the commandments, and the magisterium.

The American authorities absolutely refuse to allow me expiation for my great, but lesser, crimes in Italy and Palestine, and they keep me under surveillance at the Mount St. Alphonsus Redemptionist Sanatorium at Esopus. I write Cascais, continually, without response, wondering if my letters are posted, and wondering if the monarchists knew the truth from the beginning, fully aware of Monsignor Cottino's contention that "The Shroud is the symbol of the monarchy, especially after the war," and had, quite innocently, directed me towards Jerusalem to safeguard the Weizman discovery.

Regardless, and despite what even they might contend, my sanity remains bafflingly stable, and thus the resultant despair is, I'm certain, even the more debilitating. Even now, after so much time, the civil authorities, and even the consenting clerics, still seem totally in shock. They seem unaware that their protective charity and compassion, mistakenly founded on their inexorable conviction in a "severe mental disbalance" and thus a consequent disbelief in my own responsibility for my actions, is only the more exasperating and terrifying. And so, continually, inconsolably, from within these wretched depths, I compare my crimes to Judas and prostrate myself.

Endgame

THERE WAS AN ENCROACHING MALIGNANCY in the dark of that warm summer night. Even though it was still vague and uncertain, I somehow sensed it all before it actually happened, and I was unable to sleep. So I sat in the silence of that ancient and unsuspecting city as 250,000 armed troops invaded through four borders at twelve locations and quickly and efficiently occupied the country. At 11 PM, the Ruzyn Airport, outside the capital, was secured, and a constant stream of AN-24 transports began landing every few minutes, disgorging airborne infantry and armored military vehicles. Soon, long columns of combat troops spearheaded by countless T-34 tanks were moving toward the Hlavek Bridge, over the Vltava River, and into the center of the city.

So the capital woke in the night to the frightening sounds of invasion: rumbling tanks, the precision march of disciplined troops, and the chilling sounds of flashing MIG fightercraft. Exhausted, I took to the streets and wandered about, stunned by their audacity and fearful for the consequences. Eventually, scattered resistance surfaced throughout the city and barricades were set up around Wenceslaus Square at the heart of the capital. Just after dawn, an assault column of T-34 and T-54 tanks reached the Radio Center, and several hundred people who tried to impede the invaders' progress were fired upon. Several were hit, the barricades were smashed, and glass littered the streets.

I remember seeing a bloodstained flag rising defiantly over the rubble, and then, suddenly, right before me, a young boy was struck in the chest when a cold-blooded Kalmyk opened with his AK-47. As I moved toward the dying boy, a flaming projectile flew through the air just over my head and smashed into the turret of a moving tank. It immediately exploded in a fury of flames as its crew scrambled out to safety. Then a second nearby tank was struck, and it also burst into a fiery conflagration. As all of these flames filled the square with a dark black smoke, I again attempted to reach the wounded young boy, but I was immediately seized by three armed members of the district police. As they pulled me off the square, one of the three, sensing my concern, commented in Czech, with what seemed a rather callous and readily acquiescent resignation:

"He's dead."

I knew it was the truth, and I felt, as I had all night long, helpless and hopeless. When the same young soldier demanded my papers, I methodically produced my passport, and he studied it very carefully as a small police van drove up.

"Come with us."

It was a short ride in the back of the vehicle, and it led to a solitary cell in a formidable structure at Vrchlického Park which seemed to be the invaders' primary inner-city headquarters, and which had all the marks of a fortified camp. Exhausted and fully despairing the fate of my native country, I fell asleep on the cold hard floor of the dark and empty room.

Nevertheless, almost immediately, I was awakened by the

imposing sounds of the outside locks. The lights were switched back on, and a young Czech in civilian clothes walked into the room, accompanied by an "advising" officer from the occupying forces. The young Czech looked me over quite carefully, without expression, and I had no doubt that he was STB—Czech Secret Police.

"Identification."

I took out my passport again, and he looked it over.

"Canadian?"

When I said nothing, he spoke directly.

"We know what you are."

I had absolutely no idea what he was talking about, and I remained silent.

"You're a courier for MI5."

The absurdity of this notion was so capacious, and my own temperament so exacerbated by sleeplessness, that I responded with a firm and intended belligerence.

"I flew to Bratislava to attend my father's funeral."

"We know that."

He paused for a moment. Then, under the careful watch of the foreign officer, he continued.

"We also know your past—your illegal emigration—and we know that you stopped in Berlin before Bratislava, and that now, for no justifiable reason, you're here in Prague."

He gave me no opportunity to respond, turned to the silent officer, and they conversed briefly in Russian. Then they turned away, left the room, and the lights were extinguished. So, once again, I sat on the cold floor in the darkness, reconsidering the charges against me. Even though their accusations had absolutely no validity, my father had been a Slovakian dissident, and he was purged and imprisoned after the war. Suddenly, a chill ripped through me. I remembered that Monsignor Šindelka had given me a letter in Hlohovec. Right after my father's funeral, I'd mentioned to the pastor that I was planning to visit Prague before leaving the country, and he told me that a certain Kliment would find me at the King Charles Hotel and claim the letter. I'd thought nothing of his request at the time, but now, confined in the darkness, I felt for the letter under my coat and grew fearful, not really for my own life, which was, most probably, already forfeit, but for whomever else the letter might jeopardize if it fell into the wrong hands.

Immediately, the lights switched back on, and both men reentered the room. The Czech was clearly displeased about something, but he strove to maintain his stoic exterior. Without a word, they directed me out of my room, down many long and endlessly guarded corridors, and, finally, at last, into the busy office of a high-ranking but temporarily absent military officer. After we stood waiting for a few minutes, a heavily decorated Russian General in his late fifties entered the room and carefully looked me over. With a gesture of his hand, he dismissed his personal staff, but my own two personal escorts remained in the room. In the ensuing silence, I waited with a certain calmness of spirit in front of his desk. Finally, he pulled out my passport and spoke in Russian.

"A priest now? Living in North America?"

Since I have little facility with that particular language, the young STB officer translated. When I refused to respond to what was perfectly obvious, the Russian spoke again, and his comments were immediately translated by the young Czech.

"I saw you beat Bondarevsky."

I should have been stunned, but only those who apprehend the true depth of the Russian national passion for that meaningless pastime could comprehend how this cynical and arrogant man could take the time to initiate such a conversation in the midst of a cruel and barbaric invasion. It was a casual match I'd played as a precocious young boy. I believe I was fifteen at the time, and I was also, I suppose, a true prodigy of the game. Immediately after the final round of the Prague-Moscow Tournament in 1946, won so decisively by the Russians, Kottnauer had arranged a game with Bondarevsky. Like most Russian masters, he found foreign prodigies an amusing curiosity, and he only agreed to play since he felt himself at no possible risk. I remember, quite clearly, that I played a tenacious Sicilian Defence, caught him off guard, and won on the twenty-ninth move. He was obviously humiliated and irritated, but Kottnauer insisted that it was too late for another game, and he swept me away.

"I was there that day."

We'd played in the lobby of the Hotel Vltave, and it was full of Russians. I vaguely recalled that, in the midst of the onlookers, there was an officer in uniform who watched intently and took a particular pleasure in Bondarevsky's defeat and obvious discomfort. However, in the present moment, I chose to give the General no indication of remembering his presence, and he seemed clearly displeased. Then he looked away and seemed to change the subject.

"You're to be executed."

I waited.

"To vanish."

"These Czechs," I responded with accusation, "do *nothing* without your direction."

The Russian looked over at the young Czech who continued to translate.

Then he nodded and paused.

"I will offer you . . . an agreement."

Again, I waited.

"We'll play for your life—and your passport."

That such a callously hollow man could conceive of such an idea was not surprising to me, but I could, in no way, fathom what he would hope to gain by winning.

Then he explained:

"You will sign a letter to Bondarevsky and the Soviet Chess Federation informing them of my victory and my superior play."

He then addressed the ever-silent Russian officer who immediately went to a desk and typed up a short dictation. As he did so, the young STB officer translated its brief and perfectly direct message: that General Vernadsky had beaten me soundly in a short match and was decidedly "the superior player." The General then explained, through the young Czech, the terms of the arrangement: a best two of three, played on each of the next few nights at 11 PM. Realizing that I had no choice, and that this might allow me time to dispose of Father Šindelka's letter, I took up a pen and signed the note. Then I looked at the General.

"I should warn you; I haven't played in twenty years."

The Russian Commander smiled. I wasn't sure what it meant, but I was informed that I could have a day's practice, and that the first game would now be held on Thursday night. This gave me thirty-six hours. When this was decided, Vernadsky spoke briefly to the young Czech. It was clear to me that he wanted to keep his little arrangement quiet from his military colleagues, and I also sensed that the young Czech was not very pleased with the situation. I felt certain that this fanatical young man only wished to be done with me altogether, believing that there was much more important work to be done on the streets of the capital. Finally, the General turned my way once again and spoke in Russian, as the young Czech explained impassively.

"The General instructs me to give you whatever competition I can. The General notes that I'm a strong player, although I've never taken a game from my Russian superior."

I was immediately dismissed and then quickly escorted by the Czech, referred to as Captain Čapek, and his Russian advisor back across the shattered and occupied city to the old Czernin Palace, another obvious invasion stronghold. I was taken to a small room with a small cot, locked inside, and I fell directly to sleep until late the next day.

When I awoke from my long and deeply troubled sleep, the first thing I noticed was the small, well-crafted wooden chess set waiting on a nearby table. As the terrible realities of the night before slowly returned, the Russian agent from the previous day stood up from his chair across the room and called for my breakfast. As I rose to eat, I recalled Father Šindelka's letter, and I grew very irritated with myself for not having made an attempt to dispose of it during the night. But there was absolutely nothing I could do at the present time, and when Čapek arrived, we played several games—five in fact—and though I had not actually played in over twenty years, I drew the first and won each successive game with a progressive ascendancy. The Captain played a steady, sure, and solid chess, but rather unimaginative and especially weak in the middle.

Although I tried to initiate conversation, he generally remained silent. Whenever I pressed him for information about what was happening on the outside streets of Prague, he was unwilling to discuss the subject, and this tended to confirm my worst fears. I also hoped to learn something about Vernadsky's play, but, again, I was told nothing. That night, after supper, I chose to work board problems alone, and, although always under the surveillance of the silent Russian, I took some time to consider my circumstances and reflect on the irony of my predicament. My four convincing wins over Čapek had once again raised an old and evil specter— the very same problem that had led to my abandoning the game at the age of seventeen. "Victory" in chess, more so than victory of any other kind, tends to eradicate the possibility of personal humility, and, of necessity, it seems to conjure and exacerbate an inordinate pride.

That particular enmity, pride, I came to realize in my youth was the root of all other harms and vices, the font of misery, and the source of all modern apostasy and immorality. I came to follow Proverbs that "Pride goeth before destruction," and I realized that this warning had special application to my own personal tendency to inflated self-esteem. Even during a wild and rebellious adolescence, when I'd fascinated and even shaken up the entire Czech Chess Federation with my precocious play, I understood that, for me, at least, the game could only lead to presumption, self-absorption, and nihilism. I was somehow keenly aware of my own weaknesses, and I became convinced that such an awareness was the mark of self-understanding and the beginning of wisdom.

When I finally chose the path to the altar and the priesthood— to obedience—I found it far less difficult to abandon the game than I could ever have imagined. In 1948, on the advice of my parish priest, and with the encouragement of my loving but fearful parents, who clearly foresaw the coming coup and the coming religious persecution, I joined the Prague delegation to the Bad Gastein International Masters Tournament as an observer and then sought political asylum in Austria during the play. I was soon at seminary in Galway, and, on ordination, was assigned a small parish in the far-away Creignish Hills of Cape Breton Island. There, I worked very hard to try and bring some compassion into the world around me, and I watched with a deep and restless remorse the tragic fate of my distant fatherland.

At 10:45, Čapek, the Russian, and a young Czech guard escorted me through various corridors and courtyards to a quiet and comfortable private room. Since I'd been under watch all my waking hours, I prayed silently that the letter would continue to go undetected. The room was paneled, draped, and softly lit, and near the far high windows a chessboard and two chairs awaited the match.

We had just entered the room when the General also arrived. Instinctively, as an apparent matter of routine precaution, I was frisked by the Czech guard who found the letter. My heart and my spirit immediately collapsed. I lost all my strength, and a nausea overwhelmed me. The General took the letter, saw that it was written in Czech, and put it in his pocket. He seemed somewhat curious, but he was far more interested in the match at hand.

As we took our seats, another small table was pulled up beside the General. He took out my passport and the note to Bondarevsky, and he placed them on the table. Then taking white, without discussion, he opened Ruy Lopez, but I was unable to respond. I felt as if I'd failed in the most dreadful way, and the game now seemed perfectly meaningless. I was unprepared and totally disinterested, and I looked coldly at Vernadsky.

"What exactly are you doing in Prague?"

Concerned only with the game, the Russian was quite astonished by the impertinence of my question as it was translated by Čapek, but he smiled.

"We've established order." Then he added with a characteristic arrogance, "The city is under control. The resistance is over."

I stood up, walked over to the windows, and looked down into the dark courtyard below. I had absolutely no interest in playing games, and I knew that I couldn't proceed. Then the General, angered by the delay, made himself perfectly clear.

"You will play, or you will die tonight."

Actually, I had fully believed that my life was forfeit in either case, yet despite my deep anxieties, I still harbored the vague hope that somehow, in some way, I might salvage some good from this seemingly hopeless situation.

I returned to the table, sat down, and offered the Berlin Defense. I quickly lost the center, developing an awkward cluster in the queenside pawn group. The General was firm, tenacious, and opportunistic. As my position deteriorated, I recalled that Lasker had lost a similar line at Munich in 1908, and I attempted to neutralize my adverse situation. But every resistance proved inadequate, my strategic disadvantage was too overwhelming, and, much like Lasker at Munich, I was forced to resign at the thirty-second move.

We'd played in total silence, under the close watch of Čapek who stood nearby during the entire contest. When I tilted the black king on its side, the General stood up, and his arrogance and self-satisfaction were unbearable.

"Tomorrow, at eleven o'clock."

Then he took my passport and the Bondarevsky note, and he left the room. I sat in silence and stared at the board. I suppose I seemed to Čapek and the others in the room a rather pathetic exhibition of defeat and capitulation. Yet despite this most convincing defeat and the tragedy of the confiscated letter, I now underwent a reversal of attitude. I reasoned that I was, in most likelihood, dead already, and that my only satisfaction could come in beating this cynical and sinister agent of repression, death, and ethical apostasy. I was also now quite convinced that I could actually beat the man across the board, especially in the endgame.

Moments later, as I and my three escorts walked in silence across the dark and quiet courtyard, I suddenly realized that we were now within the Foreign Ministry Building, and that this was the exact location of the Masaryk tragedy of March 1948. I glanced up at the summer night sky above me, and I recalled the shocking end of that honest and dedicated statesman, whose fate, more than anything else, seemed to epitomize the unrelenting tragedies of this country: the Munich betrayal; the Nazi invasion, occupation, servitude, and concentration camps; the Prague uprising, the Red Army, and the Red coup; more tyranny, more terror, more purges, and more camps; and now, the present invasion.

As we crossed the enclosed square, I grew certain that this was the very courtyard where Masaryk was conveniently found dead, as Gottwald and the communists seized control of the country in the wake of the war. Masaryk had apparently fallen several stories from his private quarters, but few Czechs believed the official verdict of suicide. Somehow, I drew strength from these recollections, and determined to win the next night, not simply to satisfy my own oppressed ego, but to, in some small way, assert a national integrity against this endless stream of godless invaders. So I actually slept soundly that night, as well as any condemned man who's found within himself a certain peace and contentment and purpose.

The next day, Friday the 23rd, I chose, to Čapek's satisfaction, to prepare for the night's match alone. At 8 PM, as I took a late supper, I was astonished to discover a small note placed beneath the clutter on my serving tray. Although I was still under Russian observation, I was able to read the brief message undetected. It was written in Czech and warned: "You *must* win tonight—other lives are at stake." I was naturally astounded that such a note could be passed through an invasion stronghold, and I was equally surprised by its implication that the General actually planned to honor his promise to set me free if I won the match. Nevertheless, although I still remained doubtful of such a possibility, I was now well-rested, confident, and determined as I eventually took my chair opposite the General at 11 PM.

With white, I opened Ruy Lopez, and the General took a Russian Defense. Playing quite strong for black, Vernadsky was able to neutralize certain inherent disadvantages, and he struck for a line similar to Euwe's black victory in Budapest before the war. When the General offered a draw at the twenty-eighth move, I refused. I'd played the entire game calculated to slowly take away from his strength, with the endgame always in sight. Even as a young child, I'd taken a most unlikely and precocious interest in the endgame, and I'd worked incessantly over Tattersall's *Thousand End-Game Studies.* I believed with Nimzovitch that "eighty percent of the whole of the endgame technique rested on combined play," and this became my specialty as I soon began turning drawn positions into wins through precise preparation and concentrated execution. Although I was never able to achieve the breathtaking ingenuity of Rubinstein's flawless endgame, I soon developed so sound an ability for finish that much of my high reputation as a prodigy was actually based on a relentless and uncompromising endgame.

It was, in fact, exactly true that I'd not played competitively in over twenty years, but I'd managed to keep up with the game in spare moments, occasionally working problems over the board. And now, I was absolutely amazed at how quickly my sense of endgame combination returned in competition, especially against such a strong opponent. Vernadsky was obviously irritated by my refusal to draw, and, as his position deteriorated, his strain, frustration, and resentment intensified. Finally, worn out and furious, he tipped his king and stood over me in a defiant posture.

"You will *not* win tomorrow."

He spoke with a slow, sure confidence. Then he turned away and exited the room.

The next day, I prepared for the most important game of my life. I worked hard, practiced quickly, and reconsidered my various options. During an afternoon break from the rigors of preparation, I was, to my amazement, able to engage the silent Russian in a surprisingly candid conversation about Vernadsky. He spoke excellent Czech, and this fact, along with an obvious lack of fear for his military commander made me consider for the first time that he was not actually KGB, but rather GRU.

He told me that, as a young man, Vernadsky had always preferred chess and its society to the military life, but in a Russian Juniors' Tournament in Moscow, he was beaten off the board by his rival and cousin, Igor Bondarevsky. The match was decisive and the Kremlin apparatchiks directed him, without option, toward a military career. He rose quickly in the ranks, but he never forgot his abasement in Moscow, which Bondarevsky continually exacerbated by his absolute refusal to ever play his cousin again. Vernadsky's continual challenges were always smugly brushed off as unworthy of the Grandmaster's attention, and, in 1946, when Bondarevsky took the young Czech boy lightly in Prague and was trapped in a losing position, it was Vernadsky, a VIP spectator, who took the greatest satisfaction in the master's humiliation.

At exactly 11 PM, a very self-assured and determined Vernadsky pushed his opening pawn to king 4. I answered with Sicilian Defense: Classical Dragon, and he seemed somewhat disturbed by this rather unlikely response. That particular defense is rich in complications and "involved" positions, and I was able to force an asymmetrical pattern combined with a highly dynamic defense. I gradually moved through a seemingly even middle game toward a totally dominant ending position. I concentrated as never before, forgot everything around me, and drew on a deep and unrelenting self-confidence.

In time, deep into the night, the board was mostly clear. We stood rooks even, but I had an insurmountable three pawn edge— and two were passed. The ending was at hand and irrevocable, and, suddenly, as I recognized mate in six, a vindictive satisfaction swept over me, and I spoke through the terrible tension with an obvious self-assurance.

"Mate in six."

But the Russian paid no attention and stared intently at the board, and Čapek, clearly stunned by what he saw, refused to translate. Satisfied, I sat back in my chair. Then Čapek checked his watch, removed his Mauser semi-automatic, and walked toward the board. Stunned, I watched as he lifted his weapon high in the air over the board and slammed the gun downward into the back of the General's neck. There was a sharp, sickening crack, and Vernadsky slipped from his chair and slumped to the ground. I had no doubt that the man was dead, and, in my confusion, I could ascertain no purpose for what had happened. I then looked up at Čapek again, but he refused to take his eyes off the board. Then his hand reached out, and he moved . . .

P-K6!

Though still shocked by the ruthless efficiency of the assassination that had just taken place before my eyes, both Čapek's behavior and the unbelievable audacity of his move, forced my attention back to the game. Methodically, I gave the only possible response

. . . PxP

He then moved immediately, with an even more stunning move.

K-B6!

I responded as I must, and we quickly played out the game:

. . .	P-R3
R-R8ch	K-R2
R-R7ch	K-R1
K-Kt6	R-Kt4ch
KxP	R-Ktl
R-R7 mate!	

I stared at the board in disbelief as my "irrevocable" victory fell to ashes. Then I looked up at Čapek, who seemed rather complacent about the uncanny brilliance of his play, and I wondered if Vernadsky could have known.

"Did he see it?"

"I don't know."

Then he added:

"But he would have killed you anyway."

As I waited for an explanation, he lifted up my passport, ripped out the middle two pages, and handed it back to me. Then the Czech guard entered the room with a parcel, and I realized, for the first time, that the GRU officer was absent and must have left sometime during the match.

Čapek broke into my thoughts.

"I'm sorry to have done things this way; we had little choice."

The Czech guard dumped a Russian uniform over the chessboard, and the few remaining pieces scattered, as Čapek continued.

"We hope to have you to the border by dawn."

I rose up, put on the uniform, and then bent over Vernadsky and said a silent prayer.

"Stay with Kliment, and when you're safe at the border, he'll answer your questions."

I looked at Čapek, and he held out his hand and shook mine firmly.

"Take care, and pray for us."

The young Captain's cold exterior had momentarily passed. Suddenly, for the first time, I was able to sense the warmth and humanity beneath his habitually cool demeanor, so obviously hardened by the complexities and endless dangers of their interminable struggle for freedom.

I wondered out loud:

"Could I do any good here?"

He shook his head, but with obvious appreciation.

"Not here."

Kliment soon moved me out of the room, down endless, mostly deserted corridors, to the grim and quiet streets of the occupied and "normalized" capital. Once outside the boundaries of the city, we drove south through Jihočeský Province to České Budějovice, and then moved west through the Bohemian Forest toward the West German border. We rode in silence, had a few close scrapes, but Kliment was always unflappable and resourceful. So I found myself, for the second time in my life, riding south through Czechoslovakia toward the freedoms of the West. As we drove quickly through the clear cool night of the Czech countryside, I grew ashamed of the foolish pride to which I'd succumbed when victory seemed certain, and I prayed for forgiveness.

I also thought, at length, about the bravery and humility of that young freedom fighter, Čapek, working against all odds within the very confines of the STB. As I reconsidered the events of the evening, I felt certain that the General's body was inevitably and irrevocably fated to fall into the Foreign Ministry courtyard, and somehow, in retribution for Masaryk, would end up being officially classified a suicide.

At the border, twelve miles east of Grafenau, we left the car on a dirt road and walked ahead with the coming dawn rising behind us. The young Czech was forthright.

"You were carrying a message that, if passed, would have aided the dissident cause, but, if intercepted, could have compromised the lives of certain Slovakian freedom fighters. When the invasion took us all by surprise, even at STB, Čapek was notified by the underground. He, thus, had three immediate goals: to find you in Prague, secure the message, and get you safely to the border. Then the Russian, in signing a routine approval of prisoner transfer, recognized your name and complicated the situation. Especially when he kept your passport."

I listened in silence as we continued walking.

"You see, the crucial message was *not* in the letter, that was only a decoy; the real message was encoded into your passport. Given these complications, Čapek decided to assassinate the General; this would have been considered in any event since Vernadsky had been especially brutal in Budapest, and we feared that he might attempt the same behavior in Prague. But for many other complex and complicating reasons, the only time to successfully effect both the assassination and your escape, was at exactly two AM this morning during the changing of the guard at Invasion Headquarters. This delay was actually fortuitous since it allowed the decoy letter to cause a great deal of useful confusion in Slovakia, but when you lost the initial game that first night, the second game became absolutely crucial."

Then Kliment paused, and stopped on the path, and seemed to digress.

"I wonder, Father, do you pray when you play?"

His obvious sincerity caught me off-guard, and it caused me to reflect on my own shortcomings.

"No, but you've made me realize that I should."

He thought it over a moment, and then he continued.

"You see, there were two other men—extra-national agents— who were scheduled to be executed with you as soon as you'd lost the match."

He looked at me with a certain admiration that I certainly didn't deserve.

"You played for three lives that night, Father. Had you lost, Čapek could have done nothing."

There was an awkward silence since I was uncertain how to respond to his generosity. Finally, I changed the subject.

"Čapek plays extraordinary chess."

"Yes, I believe he does, but like you, he has other priorities."

We then continued on our way toward the western border.

"And Czechoslovakia?"

"We've certainly lost for now, but we've kept calm and maintained our hope."

I was amazed, even moved, by his perspective, his courage, and his faith. I wondered if it characterized the feelings of all his countrymen.

"Are you and Čapek in any jeopardy?"

"Not really, it's all been worked out."

We walked on with the new sun rising slowly behind us. Despite Kliment's kindnesses, I was still uneasy about my behavior in that third and, now I fully realized, meaningless game. I considered the true humility of that young Čapek who must have intentionally lost every game he'd ever played with Vernadsky— for the sake of his country. And who'd also chosen to accept four losses and a draw when we'd played three days ago, clearly to build my confidence. I recalled that only those who play the game with grace can ever truly achieve a meaningful victory, and for the rest of us, as Montaigne once pointed out, the game will truly "molest the soul."

Arriving at the departure point, Kliment stopped and pointed west into the early morning mist.

"There's freedom, Father. Good luck."

I grew sad at our parting, profoundly so, but I knew that my own personal responsibilities and obligations lay ahead and far across the Atlantic.

The young boy seemed to sense my anxiety.

"Don't worry, Father, someday others will cross this border to the east and find freedom in Czechoslovakia."

I shook his hand, blessed him in the name of the Father, the Son, and the Holy Spirit, and then moved alone into the bright new day and exhilarating freedoms of the West German half of the Bohemian Forest.

William Baer, a recent Guggenheim fellow, is the author of eighteen books including *The Ballad Rode into Town; Luís de Camões: Selected Sonnets;* and *Classic American Films: Conversations with the Screenwriters.* His short stories have been published in *The Iowa Review, Kansas Quarterly, The Chariton Review, The Dalhousie Review,* and many other literary journals. He's also a former Fulbright in Portugal and the recipient of a Creative Writing Fellowship in fiction from the National Endowment for the Arts.

www.ingramcontent.com/pod-product-compliance
Lightning Source LLC
Chambersburg PA
CBHW031102020726
47495CB00007B/2001